Smuggling Donkeys

David Helwig
Smuggling Donkeys

The Porcupine's Quill

Library and Archives Canada Cataloguing in Publication

Helwig, David, 1938–
    Smuggling donkeys / David Helwig.

ISBN 978-0-88984-294-6

    I. Title.

PS8515.E4S63 2007   c813'.54   c2007-904004-7

Published by The Porcupine's Quill, 68 Main St, Erin, Ontario NOB ITO.
http://www.sentex.net/~pql

Readied for the press by Doris Cowan.

Represented in Canada by the Literary Press Group.
Trade orders are available from University of Toronto Press.

We acknowledge the support of the Ontario Arts Council and the Canada
Council for the Arts for our publishing program. The financial support of
the Government of Canada through the Book Publishing Industry
Development Program is also gratefully acknowledged. Thanks, also, to
the Government of Ontario through the Ontario Media Development
Corporation's Ontario Book Initiative.

to my old friend
David Lewis Stein

Who do you talk to when you're alone?

What Laura asked me, and I was unable to give her a smart answer. She comes up with these things to stump me. I don't, I might have said, alone's alone. Not true. Babble always. As now. Too sharp for me, that Laura. She makes my head ache.

Wherever she is.

Any chance she'll be the one stumped if she toddles back and finds me denned up in this place? Some have enlightenment forced upon them. She said she's not coming back, but maybe she'll get bored with Truth. She gets bored with things. Yesterday in the mail forwarded to me here I got a postcard of an elephant. She sends her postcards to our old address. No idea that I've run off. Think of her, bedecked with jewels and flowers, on the back of the shunting trunked grey beast.

It started with yoga, a lifetime back when we were still in Toronto where I was teaching kids in a downtown high school, and she was finishing up her degree and getting gigs as a substitute teacher, and we were thinking it was a cheerful thing to have a regular income but missing the late nights and sublime unpredictability of life in the theatre – what there was of theatre in those days – and she found Kumar Ghosh giving his weekly yoga classes upstairs from a barber on Queen Street. I'd find her on the floor of our little apartment knotted into the lotus position, breathing. She was always keen on the breathing and that led to the noises. I don't think any regulation yoga practitioner would have gone for the noises – pure theatre they were, begun with hints from some teacher of voice production. Relaxing the diaphragm. When one of Laura's groups at the night school got going it was scary. Orgiastic. Inuit throat singers too far out on the ice singing away death. Echoes of butchery. Carnage. A production of *The Bacchae* gone wicked. Rhythmic gutturals, deep bass groaning, then the soprano wails, the slurping and juddering and trills. Sometimes men decided to take her *Yoga and Free Expression* class, but they didn't last long. Men are a little tight-assed, Laura always said. Women loved the class. Maenads. Amazons.

Laura makes soft elephant grunts to communicate to the animal that carries her into the forest. In a quiet glade she will find a small building which is the newest call centre offering technical support to airline passengers wishing to book tickets. She will ride her elephant among them and trample their PCs in the name of spiritual enlightenment.

What do you see in the dark? she wanted to know. What do you hear in the silence?

Guess where I am, Laura. Guess what I've been up to.

Who do you talk to when you're alone?

Awake in the night, my not uncommon state, and more so lately, one of the little tricks of body chemistry, a greed for consciousness, now when the existence of consciousness may any day be threatened. Turn on the little light with a pink shade, picked up at a second-hand store for just this purpose, and grab up the book or notebooks lying on the floor beside the mattress, then, head banked on two pillows, the bedcovers all sluttish and betwisted, throw them around, kick them into order, scan a bit of *Hamlet* or inscribe a few clever thoughts, or stare up at the cracks in the plaster of the ceiling and search for shapes, what mothers teach their frightened children to do for comfort. Yes, very like a whale. Wish for the easeful sound of autumn rain. For someone lying on the other half of the mattress complaining about being kept awake by the light. Turn off the switch and recite verses, a way of putting the mind through its paces, metre, rhyme – *I wandered lonely as a cloud ... So we'll go no more a-roving so late into the night ... When in disgrace with fortune and men's eyes ... A bunch of the boys were whooping it up in the Malemute Saloon ...*

Morning: eyes open to see the light of day, a patch of sunshine on the distant wall, blurry until I find my specs and drop them on the available hooks, ears, nose, and watching that projected geometry of sun on world, try not to recall the first morning after she was gone, waking and turning to the other side of the bed expecting to find an ear or an open mouth or a breast hanging out of the covers, lovely old bag of fat and juices, and there was no one, nothing but light fallen from the long window with leaded panes, set high up in the wall in the room that wasn't meant to be a bedroom but perhaps a dining room, but where we had chosen to sleep, leaving a bedroom upstairs as a studio for Laura, plywood on folding sawhorses for a work surface and a bright patterned rug on the floor where her body stretched and bent, a mirror on the wall, where she would look at herself and mumble, *Elephant arse*, exaggerating the plumpnesses of middle age, always of two minds about the body, wanting to be skinny as a fakir, yet proud of her big breasts as she brought them to me.

Beyond the door is space and stairs mounting up to another space, with the tall arched windows, the pointed shape to draw the eyes upward, to heaven I suppose. Whatever is above. Odd idea, above. There is none, except in us and how we're built to stand upright on the globe. Space is curved and multidimensional and infinite and comes back around to get you from behind. A boot in the elephant arse.

Evening, and I walk up the street a block or so, turn east and make my way down the sloping gravel road to the bank of the river. On the far side, perhaps thirty feet away, stands a patch of bulrushes, and a red-winged blackbird posed on the top of one of the long brown seed pods at the top of the stem. Tomorrow the blackbirds will flock and vanish over the horizon, going south. I stand on the west bank of the river, and the setting sun is behind me, the smooth surface of the running water darkened by leaved patterns of tree shade. What colour is water when it doesn't refract the light or reflect the sky? No colour, invisible. The canoe that slid by has left no trace. The water level goes down late in summer, but with the early autumn rains it rises again. A fish dimples the surface. There is a universe of aquatic life beneath the gleaming surface, from microscopic plants to predatory pike. On the electric wires that stretch from pole to pole over the road, a fishing lure is tangled, a few feet of line hanging from it, curling in the tiny

9

evening breeze, residue of an incompetent cast by someone fishing from where I stand. At my feet, mud, prints of rubber boots going close to the edge. To my left a stand of Joe-Pye weed. Not far downstream from here the river empties into the lake. A slight sound of the current brushing the green banks. These are consoling sights and sounds. Perhaps Laura will bathe in the holy corrupted water of the Ganges. I could strip off my clothes and slide into this cool dark stream and let it carry me to the great lake.

Remember what it was like, the beginning of each school year. All those new young faces strangely like all the other young faces over the decades. A few enemies hiding out in their classrooms and offices. Laura and I were not team players, Laura worse even than I was, a sharp tongue, many opinions, no respect for pieties old or new – the vicious principles of vice principals seeking whom they might devour. The foregathering of little tongue-clackers, and hidden in other corners, old pals who could remember when smoking was a friendly communal activity. Busy Bill in his science lab surrounded by his invisible spirits, gravity and magnetism, quarks and strings, angler in the Black Holes, explicator in simple terms of what was beyond beyond, a bent man with feverish eyes, still longing for a fag, afraid of retirement. I'd given up directing plays five years ago. Couldn't say why, except it was time for someone else. Student actors have their good points, and their limits.

Each year now we saw more cheerful young faces among the staff, unformed, unmarked by life, full of schemes for our betterment. Then it was all over, and the house was crowded with the two of us, planning to stay late in bed but unable to, bumping into each other as we tried to make breakfast in the little kitchen, buying bicycles for short forays about the town and country, including the day I noticed a For Sale sign on this place. We knew everyone, but we were part of nothing, Laura getting more restless by the day.

Is this the endgame? Am I about to start my last series of moves? I was once long ago cast to play Hamm in a production of Beckett's

play, for a new experimental theatre, a room up a steep staircase
on a back street just off Yonge, around the corner from the
communist bookstore, but we only managed a single read-through
before the project fell apart. Struggling to create a new world, but
ahead of our time. Toronto wasn't ready for us. The landlord
demanded the rent, but we didn't have the rent. The producer
asked the actors if they could contribute – nothing to give. That
was the end of *Endgame*. I would have been good in that. I had a
feeling for it, Hamm, in his blindness and disease, a hampered and
fractured Oedipus, a paralyzed Lear, blind and unable to leave his
chair, comic and yet filled with some great desire that might be
love or only despair. Something. Deep.

That was during the 1960s, but before they became 'the
Sixties'. I still wore a shirt and tie to auditions. Maybe the new
world had started in San Francisco. Not in Toronto.

On the floor at the end of my rumpled bed, boxes, one with
underwear, one with socks, one with shirts, another with assorted
garments, everything still in the boxes I carried to the car when I
was abandoning our house before the auction. Important papers
are stowed in the refrigerator. On the stove one pot and one frying
pan. For lunch Kraft Dinner and fried sardines. Hanging on the
wall above the mattress, posters from a couple of my old school
productions. In the Sunday school room outside the door, a trunk
full of things I never look at.

My radio blasts out brass climaxes, symphonic traffic pile-ups.
Beethoven raging like a spurned blacksmith, and what percussion,
what great tunes will I endeavour? What is the lived equivalent to
the Fifth Symphony? Breaking things? Running amok? I think I've
never got straight what's inside the head and what's not inside the
head and how x becomes y. How, on stage, for moments, another,
imagined world occurs in the space left for it to occur. The first
world mere hypothesis.

Things come to me here. Empty space summons them.
Animals snuffling beneath the boards. Lord Skunk. Monsieur Rat.
The Duchess of Mouse and all her little hangers-on. One morning

last month I found two unknown kids sleeping on the floor upstairs. Just old enough to have run off and be travelling together. They found the church door open and put their knapsacks beneath their heads and slept side by side, and as I came on them the baby faces were empty, as sleeping faces are. It was a thought to teach with, the purity of those faces, but that's all done. I am in retirement. Laura rides her holy beast by the holy river. I fed the kids milk and cookies and sent them on their way.

Warm nights of summer, the rented chairs set on the risers, young apprentices who weren't paid enough to find a room sleeping in corners, packed two to a bag. During the day I drove down all the back roads of the district tacking up posters on hydro poles or leaving them at the motels and golf courses and occasional stores, then went on foot down the main street of town taping them up in any window that would accept one, and then in the evening I opened the box office, which meant sitting at the picnic table by the church door with the cashbox. It took me back a thousand years to my days acting in stock and one year discovering Laura. In Kingston, an hour or so away from here, there's a real theatre doing musicals. They got most of the tourists. Now and then as I sat at my table customers arrived, bought tickets. After the first week Smiler asked if he could borrow a few dollars to pay salaries, and I couldn't say no.

On the way to Christy's store for milk and eggs, I observe Amelia Schubert's wide garden, tomatoes ripening on the vines, leaves beginning to die back, brown and curling, a few fresh green ones at the top, and the plump sexy fruit hanging bright red in the late afternoon sun, a row of carrots with feathery green tops and the dark red leaves of beets, rows of flowers blooming among the veggies, zinnias, cosmos, the last brightness awaiting death by frost. Amelia, bent among them, at some obscure gardening work, waves to me. Her son played the Captain in my production of *The Sound of Music*, handsome as Christopher Plummer, like him not much of a singer, but that was fine. I have a history in this place, not a bad one, and I am imprisoned in it. That's the problem with doing your best; it reminds you that your best was decency and hard work. Oh yes, I know why Laura felt impelled to run away.

Once round the corner I pass Mary Bennett's tall Victorian pile, a tower room on the top where we liked to imagine some Upper Canadian madwoman peering out, a local Mrs Rochester. Young Philip Bennett is raking the lawn, and all at once I can smell burning leaves – a visit to my grandfather's small town one Thanksgiving weekend, a neighbour with a pile of dried leaves on fire at the curb of the empty street, smoke rising in autumn air, drifting into sunshine, the acrid smell spreading through the neighbourhood. Years now since we have been allowed to burn leaves. Keeping us safe from something. Wildfires or air pollution. Philip waves to me and I wave back. When I turn left at the next corner I will see Christy's, two or three high school boys gathered on the sidewalk outside. There is a larger grocery store in the little mall on the edge of town, and I used to drive there to load up for the week, but Christy's is closer to my current abode, and I'm all too aware that Bun and Sue Christy stay open seventeen hours a day seven days a week, in a desperate struggle to stay in business, selling mostly cigarettes to the unregenerate, lottery tickets to those crazed by hope, and odd bits of things that people decide they need close to midnight, safety pins, Tampax, a frozen pizza, milk for the next morning's breakfast. In Quebec they'd be able to sell beer and wine, and that would make their life easier. But they're not in Quebec.

In the forest schools, the students sit around their teacher and listen, and beyond in the jungle endless time speaks only to itself about its own perfection.

There's no fool like an old fool. They used to say that. Back in the days. The remnants of the oral tradition with all its mnemonic tricks, condensation, rhyme. Maxim, adage, precept. Things my grandmother said. Sure as God made little green apples. It never rains but it pours. Man proposes, God disposes. Now it's all jokes from the TV. Chatroom formulas. I don't speak any of the available languages.

Will you change the name to The Apple Orchard? I said to Tessa as she sat beside me on the picnic bench one evening in late May, and I noticed the long curling eyelashes, how the upper and lower tangled together in the corner of the eye. Just beyond the apple orchard is a short street, part of a subdivision that was supposed to expand and take over the rest of the land, but that project fell through and the orchard is neither farmed nor torn up. The apple trees all around in blossom that day, though unpruned for years, never sprayed with insecticide or fungicide, they produce small, distorted, wormy fruit. Could be used for cider or apple jelly if a person had the aptitude for such saving work. Waste not, want not, another adage from the days of scarcity. Now there is plenty in our corner of the globe. Plenty and more plenty. Factory farms shipping out multitudinous bags and crates of produce. Starvation otherwheres.

Inside the head of a lovely woman is only a fidgety brain like your own. It is not the place to go looking for mystery.

Laura will come back and tell me.

Not.

My Dog Eats Nuts. Written in boldface type across Tessa's chest when she came to the door of the house in that skimpy basketball shirt, thin muscular bare arms and shoulders, unshaven armpits, nipples of her little breasts poking against the fabric. Back after nearly ten years. Buy the old church and make me a theatre, she said, that's what it amounted too, though she presented facts, plans, personalities. Yes, I said, yes. I wanted a cliff to jump off, and here was my chance. Don't regret it. Laura was gone to the holy men and elephants, never to return, and I wandered around the house being retired and bored and trying to think what to plan for the future. How to start a new world. Wanted to be used. My own kind of asceticism and renunciation, to abandon myself to the whims of a clever woman.

How I wandered around the house in the days after Laura went: in the little back porch that was my workroom, I sat at the table in front of the windows that looked over the small back lawn to the next street, large maple trees bare against the watery blue of the spring sky, the laptop, which had crashed terminally and not been revived, pushed to one side, in front of me a pad of lined paper and a Pilot Hi-Tecpoint V7 Fine in my fingers, planning to write a play, but no words came, only a few irrelevant doodles, a little scribbled sketch of Laura, but it wasn't much like her really, and I tore it off and threw it in the wastebasket, replaced the top on the pen and put it away in my pocket, scurried to the front room and sat in the platform rocker, platform rocking for a while, and I speculated on burning the house down for the insurance, but they'd catch me, I knew, not much suited to be a criminal, and as I platform rocked, I recited dark words from the Scottish play, in which I'd played the lead, not badly for a kid, in a high school production long ago. I looked around at the walls of the house that Laura and I had bought together, where we had raised our son, shouted at each other, laughed at each other, paid off the mortgage. But now it was mortgaged again, so Laura could take her share and put it out at interest as a little something to add to her pension, not a great pension since she'd had to wait a few years to get on full time and had taken years off when Griff was born. Still too young for the government pay-out. I hoped she didn't starve or get sick out there in the holy places. When I looked around me I felt a hapless rage. No elephants came to me teaching elephant wisdom.

No, I didn't burn down the house, but when the day came to move out, I heaved it all – dishes, furnishings, books. I took with me a stick or two of furniture, a few clothes, a trunk of souvenirs, and the rest was auctioned off. I didn't watch. Laura had challenged me to this renunciation, and I had accepted the challenge.

The hunter's moon rising golden above the bent limbs of the orchard, crooked branches growing crooked apples as I walk between the rows of trees and breathe the apple-scented air. My hip aches. There was a crooked man who walked a crooked mile. Last summer, the week before opening, I sat under a full moon

15

beside Tessa and Smiler on the picnic bench by the front door as the two of them ran lines. I asked Tessa why she wasn't playing one of the bigger roles, and she said she wanted Charlotta because she loved the line *My dog eats nuts* and wandering about the stage munching a cucumber. In the darkness a whippoorwill cried loudly from the woods across the road. Smiler didn't know what it was. The moon was brilliant, perfectly round, sailing in the darkness of space, stars nearby obliterated by its light. Tessa began to recite the speech that begins *I have no proper passport. I don't know how old I am,* the words tripping by until she reached the lines *I long to talk so, and I have no one to talk to,* and then she stopped, and there was only the sound of a car in the distance. Her voice had grown deeper in the years since I had directed her on the stage of the high school. I had never been sure if I knew the meaning of the word *plangent,* but I thought it must be the word for her voice as she spoke these lines. I stood up and went back into the old church. The lights were off, but the moonlight shone through the window across the scaffolding where the lighting instruments were hung, and onto the sleeping bag by the far wall of the room, and I watched how the bag swelled and subsided with the movement of the two young bodies inside. The holy communion of the deconsecrated, I thought to myself and went down the stairs to my mattress.

Who do you talk to when you're alone? That night – Anton Pavlovich Chekhov, who thought *The Cherry Orchard* was a funny play. One kind of laughter, Anton Pavlovich, I said. Then the babble of voices began again in my head.

Imagine God (or Buddha or Krishna) looking down on all this. Warren Thouless, recently retired teacher, long-retired actor, aspiring thinker, stuffed up in a small basement room that fell into disorder. Escape suffering, or learn love, or give yourself up to unity with the cosmos, the observing Being would tell the man. Inscribe on the bare walls of your spirit the multitude of saints, the chaste and purged lovers of light, the drunken and ithyphallic angels of flesh. Grow wise. And the man would respond that he was doing his level best. Waiting for an e-mail from Burgess's Big God, but lacked a functioning laptop, desktop, Blackberry or suitable brain. It was not a problem to be solved by iteration.

Laura in the summer season of our youth – props and one small part – coming to me naked in the hot afternoon, her breasts floating, cantilevered above the little waist and the flesh of her flesh catching the light from the window of the boathouse, nineteen years old and on the new pill, and I was an older man of twenty-three, and she was daring me, the others getting into the motorboat, shouting for us, then saying leave them to it, and the boat roared, and we roared. No one to tell this to now she has run away, Griff, our one child, in Alberta in a permanent sulk like all of them out there, blaming me because his mother has run off to join some ashram or lamasery, to live on leaves and roots and wash in cold water. I wash in a small sink, strip to my aches and pains and splash all that clear water over me and scour my pale skin to bring blood to the surface.

Smiler never paid me back. Who ever believed he would?

Tubby Bert comes to discuss the taxes. Or so he says. They won't sell it out from under me yet, but he works at the township hall and he's a friend, feels worried about me because I've been deserted by my wife and am making a fool of myself, going down into the lower depths of eccentricity.
Sample conversation.
'You don't think she'll turn up one of these days.'
'Laura does what she says. I learned that when she was nineteen.'
'You been together that long?'
'Yup.'
'You always seemed happy enough.'
'At least she hasn't left me for another man.'
'A bit old for that.'
'Laura won't be too old for that when she's a hundred.'

'Another three months and you'll be in arrears. Officially.'

'I need to pay off the roof and the furnace and last summer's power bill, but I'm getting there.'

'You've got your pension.'

'I've got my pension, but I put money into the renovations last summer, and then the roof started to fly off and the furnace wouldn't start in the fall and so the money goes.'

'You didn't make too much on that Cherries thing.'

'Bad year for tourists.'

'Tourists want a comedy.'

'It's a comedy. The author said so.'

'Didn't sound very funny what I heard about it.'

'You didn't come.'

'We go out to the lake.'

'You have a regular kind of life.'

'I went to this church when I was a little guy. It was still a church in those days.'

'You were an Anglican?'

'Choirboy.'

'Pure clear tones.'

Falsetto – '*Glory be to the father and to the Son and to the Holy Ghost as it was in the beginning is now and ever shall be world without end Amen.*'

'Bert, you astonish me.'

'I astonish myself.'

'Tell me, Bert, what is a man to do?'

'His best.'

'You leave me speechless.'

'You've never been speechless in your life, Warren. Down at the curling rink you never stopped talking.'

'Maybe I've reached the age of renunciation.'

And so on.

I talk because I can't figure out what to say.

Just as the sun vanishes over the horizon, I wander through the trees of the darkening orchard, pick an apple and bite into the hard sweet flesh, grateful that the light is too dim for me to see the traces of worms, to imagine that additional protein in the fruit. Whatever it is I'm eating it is sweet to the taste. I recall the days of late spring, walking here, the branches covered with pale blossoms and the air heavy with the sound of bees as they buried themselves in each little flower and as an accidental product of their feeding, touched pollen to the female part and left the blossom fertilized, ready to bear fruit. By the time I return to the empty church, the air is growing black, and I can see the first star.

I took my copy of Hamlet upstairs, and I recited all the soliloquies, one after another, this too too sullied(?) solid(?) flesh and on to all the others. Seven of them to be placed variously about the nave, church, whatever you call such an the empty room, wondering if I might fill it with myself. Myself and Hamlet. Myself and Shakespeare. Myself and some god, though the old one has been sent packing from this house of worship. Too expensive to keep up. Deconsecrated. No longer sacred, holy. Whatever that may be. Hamlet seems alternately a believer and not. He can imagine it all, both ways. Speaking all those words I danced about the room like a young man. This too, too solid flesh. Yes, I like that reading better. Enough corruption in the play as it is. I never played Hamlet. Or even First Gravedigger. Instead of keeping the appointment for my Stratford audition I married Laura. If I auditioned, I thought, probably the best I could hope for was bits, to play as cast. Yet there was something in me, something grand – yes, I believe that. Instead, Laura. Something grand. One hot summer in stock then secret meetings in my basement room on Bathurst, since she was a student, lived at home in Lawrence Park, and her parents were proper, didn't know she'd bravely put herself on the pill and was screwing me night and day. I had a bad winter for work, a bit of radio, a little TV, no stage after *Endgame* fell through, the company I worked for part-time, cleaning offices, went broke, I even had to borrow money from Laura to buy food. I was, I suppose, defeated by this, my belief that I had the talent to make my way, that any price was worth paying so that the world could watch me on the stage, hear me speak, was insufficient. Never to be Hamlet. My father was unwell, diabetes and recurrent pneumonia. My mother was never altogether well, or so it seemed, though she outlived him by many years, went on and on surviving, not complaining most of the time, but maintaining a too-stoic silence. I suppose my will was broken, but as a compensation, I had Laura and our endless and inventive appetites. Delighted flesh, a broken will. I went back to university and became a schoolteacher, theatre my avocation, a little acting locally, directing student shows, and one or two of my students considered throwing themselves into the dangerous business of the acting life. A few old friends had made a go of it. And that was life when Tessa came along, talent boiling up in her, boiling over. I recall a night of one-act plays when she directed herself in something that was half-mime, half-dance, a performance to the recording of L. Cohen's 'Famous Blue Raincoat'. That's what she wore, with a black body stocking underneath, long pale hands touching her own lips, body. Beautiful moody sex with Leonard. I'd observed a tendency for her skin to break out along the edges of her dark hair, which was, for this performance, cut short to match Cohen's in a well known photograph. I'd observed too that her fingernails were, on occasion, not perfectly clean. I'd observed that she had a talent verging on the prodigious. What she did could have been silly, but wasn't. She managed to catch the tone, wheedling, brave, paradoxical, above all intimate. Moved as if she were naked. Another time she recited 'The Raven' to the accompaniment of herself playing a small drum. The audience giggled once or twice. She had ideas and was willing to take terrible chances. It was all she cared about. She had a boyfriend for a while, one Terry Grace, a pleasant tall boy who said he admired her, but he objected to the revelations of the blue raincoat, and may even have been one of those who giggled at 'The Raven', and she sent him packing. I followed her progress after she dumped Terry and went on to theatre school, began to get work, but even with her level of ability it is a hard road. She is not yet famous. She came to me for help. There's a divinity that shapes our ends. Well, maybe.

As a librarian watched with professional detachment, Warren
Thouless sat at a long table in the public library with the
Encyclopedia Britannica open in front of him at the article on
India, more than 160 pages, complete with long bibliographies,
beyond that a section on the Indian ocean with its islands and a
long discussion of Indian philosophy. Warren, as he sat there,
turning the leaves forward and back, appeared to be overwhelmed
by the endless fact after fact, transliterated Indian words long and
unpronounceable, by all they tried to tell him about this
subcontinent in which his wife had chosen to lose herself, with no
hint about where in the complex geography with its mountains and
plains and rivers and tribes and castes and varying complexions,
dark Dravidians in the south, pale Aryans in the north, 723
languages and dialects, mysterious observances, Indian elephants
in the rain-sodden forests of Assam, that one small human figure
might lurk. Could anyone imagine how she had decided where to
go? Absurd: suppose a political refugee from Kashmir, speaking no
English, was to set off for Canada, aiming himself at the particular
town in eastern Ontario where Warren sat in the small public
library, flummoxed, astray in the spaces of possibility. Take, with
the attendant librarian, a god's-eye view of Warren's smallness and
irrelevance and at the same time his afflicting recognition of
absence, his wife lost in some spiritual community too small to be
seen on the hugest map, infinitesimal, and she a dot within the
smallest dot, and he couldn't recall the name of the place, had no
idea of the latitude or longitude, no comprehension of any of the
dialects spoken in the great cities or the mountain villages, except
that familiar lilting version of English with its precise ticking
consonants. He knew the names of only one or two of the many
gods, which, he read, were all one god. Even the stamps on the
postcards she sent were alien to him – the exotic, the picturesque,
as we all know, a delusion, a way of taming the absolutely foreign,
the inapprehensible, and making it small, delightful, something to
be transported, framed and hung on the wall, when in fact India is
as black and far away as death.

At the library counter the tall slender man with slightly
protuberant eyes, a former student, who, when Warren arrived,
called him Mr Thouless and smiled, observed Warren as he slogged
through the paragraphs, making notes on a lined pad, to no
purpose except to keep his mind alert, or perhaps to prevent
himself from screaming. Noted that the man mumbled to himself
as he read. Roman traders, the pages told him, arrived somehow in
the first century of the Common Era (Year of Our Lord) though
long after the Jains had invented non-violence and Buddha had
risen from his quiet place under a tree and announced that
suffering arose out of craving, craving out of sensation, sensation
out of contact – the word which was usually translated *suffering*
meaning both pain and pleasure – and how by following certain
rules it might be possible to get off the recurring wheel of
reincarnation and sit still. Perhaps Warren's vanished wife would
get off the wheel while he himself would be reincarnated as an
aardvark or polecat. Warren, though a teacher of history, had never
studied or taught Indian history except as an adjunct to the history
of Britain, colonial administration in the eighteenth and nineteenth
centuries, independence in the twentieth. He riffled the pages as
one who struggled with the accumulated unrealities of the other
kingdom into which his wife had vanished. The cycle of gods went
on, creator, sustainer, destroyer; this provoked a philosophical
vertigo. Perhaps controlled breathing, counting ten in, ten out,
would keep off hysteria.

The librarian, part time here, the rest on the road opening
other branches for a few hours here and there, watched his former
teacher, the lips moving, singing to himself, you might say. He had
been told that the man's wife had left him, and he wondered if this
was a first step in some serious deterioration. Warren Thouless had
been a good teacher, and the librarian observing his growing
eccentricity felt a certain regret.

I found a package of dried peas on a shelf at Christy's, covered
with dust, but a dried pea is meant to last for decades, and they had
some sliced ham, and onions to be weighed out, and I have cooked

them all together, pea soup. New and larger saucepan for the endeavour: Christy's has one of everything. The soup smells good.

November today. Darkest month of all the darknesses. Difficult to propel myself into the grey imitation of daylight.

This morning there is snow on the ground, the first of the year. Not likely to stay, but an omen. It is beautiful, lying lightly on the world, and yet it fills me with apprehension. I wonder if I will survive the winter in this bare stone edifice. The summer kept me busy, it all made sense, but now there is too much silence. I must write a play, or act in one. I planned to go out and buy a newspaper this morning, sit and read it over coffee, but I find I am afraid of what disasters the columns of black and white letters will report. There are days when I think we ought to have had more children, five or six, so that every day one or other might be calling with some kind of news or request. But they would, even a dozen of them, have separate and complex lives, as alien to mine as Griff's out there in the west.

It was the night that Tessa did her Blue Raincoat performance that I first met her parents. When I chatted to her after rehearsals it was not about her family but about the future – what plays we might perform, what she might do after high school – but there were rumours of a pair of intense back-to-the-landers coming down out of the high country to meet her teachers annually on the night set up for such endeavours. As they came toward me outside the auditorium, her father looked fierce enough, a moustache and broad shoulders, but when they introduced themselves he proved to be soft-spoken, still a trace of the North Carolina accent he'd grown up with as he asked whether the Blue Raincoat thing was my idea. All her own, I assured him, and he said, Yes, he'd expected that. She was a girl given to ideas. The mother had clear, precise features like Tessa's, nice straight nose, wide brow, with a lot of thick hair above it, wild and about the colour of a moose, something rawboned about her by comparison with her girl, maybe

23

just age and outdoor work, and she asked if I thought Tessa had a chance of making a living in the theatre, what she was determined to do. Hard, I said, hard for anyone to make a living, but I believed she had real talent and courage, and how could she not have courage, I thought as I spoke, being the daughter of a man who'd fled the draft and then stayed, subsistence farming in some corner of the woods north of here. I couldn't advise anyone to try to make a life of acting, I said, since I'd made the attempt and abandoned it, but I thought her chances of theatre school were excellent, and beyond that, who was to know? The mother met my eyes and held them, the way Tessa sometimes did, and she said, She thinks the world of you. And I of her, I said, but I've told her it's a hard world, too much for me when I was young. Though it's better now; there's more going on, movies here and there.

Parents worry. It goes with the job. And obviously there wasn't a lot of money, but as the mother said, turning to go, I guess we did what we wanted, and she will too. And she did, and part of what she wanted was to do *The Cherry Orchard* in this old church. No knowing what she'll want next.

Morning, abed, I decide to take my text of *Hamlet* in hand and go up to the body of the church, where I have seven positions, one for each soliloquy. Lying on my mattress, planning this private performance, I conclude that the play is defined by the choice of soliloquy as the key to its rhetoric. William Shakes grabbed hold of the old play, Kyd or whoever, and had the bright idea of plump Dick Burbage giving a bunch of speeches standing alone onstage. Playwrights had done it – *Rex solus dixit* – but never before so inveterately, so much the play's habit. Once that formal decision was made, I realized – turning over on the mattress, pulling the covers across my shoulders, crushing an incipient erection – the play became a triumph of *the pale cast of thought*, subjectivity, and Hamlet's postponements, his neurotic playing with himself, were the imperatives.

First position, at the top of the stairs, to one side of the great wooden doors, liturgical west (in fact south southwest at best) and

I open the book. It is a young man's part, a young man's play, but I am in no mood for Lear or Prospero, wish to inhabit the restless subjectivity of the black prince. Hamlet hasn't yet seen the Ghost, but his skin itches with the creep of weeds in this untidy garden, obsessed with the appetite of his mother for the bodies of men, father, uncle, impatient to be humped by one king or his replacement. I read out the words, clearly, largely, sound bouncing off the walls into the emptiness. *But break my heart, for I must hold my tongue*, he ends, but of course he doesn't hold his tongue but talks and talks and talks, and we in the audience are trapped in a sickened mind.

Cross the space to the far wall and move forward in the nave. *Remember me*, the ghost has said, and departed into ghostland, (played by Will S. his own self, the gossip says) and the young fella swears how perfectly he will remember what he has been told. Has known his mother's itch, but now, the ghost tells him that his father was murdered, the old poison-in-the-ear trick. Never fall asleep in the orchard. And Hamlet begins to be stuck in the goo of his own metaphors – notebook of memory, then out of the pocket with his little commonplace book – writes it down, *that one may smile and smile and be a villain*, and we see how he gets himself into the spiderweb of phrases, always tempted like a poet to take the word for the act.

Cross again and augment, and now we move from words to theatre, the player's passion, actor's tears, and Hamlet accuses himself of silence, and mere words, which are an existential silence, curses and accuses himself of cowardly evasion. I speak it bravely, baritone of the mid-range echoing from stone and wood and back to my own musical ears. Mind at its desperate worst, seeing itself being itself, person as subject and object, the will's simplicity baffled by awareness.

The centre, equidistant from north and south, east and west, halfway from door to altar, wall to wall, and here the stale words to be made new, TB or not TB; how is any actor to pronounce it, that absolute moment of selfhood when Hamlet is propelled by the knowledge that he might turn the will against the thing whose will it is? No greater challenge to an actor than to make the words fresh when he knows that the audience is singing along, at least half of them knowing the lines he speaks before he says them. The temptation to break up the phrases, make them jagged, incoherent in a desperate attempt to achieve freshness. How simple, the words tell us, not to exist at all, the life abused so easily abandoned. And then at the end Ophelia appears, pretty thing, and Hamlet's pretence of madness begins more and more to tip over into the real thing, sex-hate, the self, in which he is so entangled, losing all the delicate adjudications of perception and response, the pretty thing to be fouled, punningly called cunt, hurt, cast off for the sake of some freedom which is a whirling dementia.

Hide in the farthest corner, behind the line of altar, back to the wall, voice on stone. No further to go, the witching time of night, and he prepares in some muddled way to confront his mother, and then trapped in the darkest corner he watches the king at his prayers and makes this his excuse not to kill, lest he send him to heaven, the altarplace the invisible presence of the king, one excuse after another, perhaps it is unnatural to kill, or it shows only the playwright who's on to a good thing not wanting to give it up, this obsessive, brilliant thinking-out-loud, the audience waiting, waiting, waiting, for the orgasm of slaughter.

At last in the position of the lost altar, the final soliloquy, and yet nothing final in it. Hamlet has killed Polonius, and even so he flannels on about his own hesitation, the fact of facts being that we perhaps can't ever act from choice of action, but only on an unthinking impulse. Hamlet has been set free from the mere habits of living but can't find the next step, whatever dance you do to the sound of no music. This is the altar of the emptied church, where will is no more than wish, wish no more than whim, the world of the individual who is only aware of himself as being an atom, has lost all the chains of necessity and belief, slopping through irony like mud in spring, the legs slow, the soul gone walkabout.

Speaking all these, one after another, leaves me depleted. I go down to heat up some leftover soup.

* * *

Hamlet, *whose mind is a complete universe in itself,* saith Dr Frye.

The trees of the orchard have caught the heavy flakes of snow, and
the black shapes are outlined in white, a new blossoming. Under
the summer blossoms I sat with Tessa, our backs against a tree,
and watched the evening sun shining through the branches, so that
each blossom, veined and tinted with pink, was a tiny lantern
holding and giving back the light, and down at the end of the row,
the sun was blindingly bright and at the core of the illumination I
caught a glimpse of a figure, in a garment of white veined with fire,
and I pointed, not speaking, and Tessa followed my gaze along the
aisle of trees, and we watched in silence until the sun fell and there
was only a misty gloaming. The figure brought with it a memory –
I was very small, my mother walking toward me on a long flat
sandy beach. I said nothing. Tessa said nothing. We had seen the
goddess whose sport is creation, destruction.

Here is a map of the town. Begin with the river that flows along the
eastern edge of the place and makes its end at the lakeshore, a half
mile below the main street. As you drive in on the old highway
from the east, you cross a bridge and see the attractive nineteenth-
century stone cottage, now owned by a lawyer named Barry
Engelhart, who regards himself as the local squire, his house full of
antique furniture, a defender of the old ways and an accumulator
of stories, real and imagined. His main practice is in Kingston, an
hour away, but he will invite a few favoured local clients to meet
with him in his parlour, overlooking the green lawn running down
to the river. Along the main street, you find two empty stores, and
one – antiques and collectibles, as they call various bits of junk –
that opens only Saturdays in the wintertime. A small insurance
agency, a small real estate office beside it. A hairdresser's shop, and
Annette Zelikovics, who runs it, will cut men's hair if you drop in
and she isn't busy. Halfway along the street the township hall – the
building that used to be the town hall before local governments
were shuffled together. Then a combination drug store and gift

shop. Billy Mundt's pizzeria next door to the now empty hotel. Jane Kravchuk's women's clothing store, with higher-quality merchandise than you would expect, or so Laura told me. At the far end of the street a liquor store. Laundromat behind it. Beside that the United Church. Tim Hortons past that, a block above Tim's a small curling rink and a public school with a big baseball diamond.

If you turn south you will pass by two or three blocks of houses, mostly small and built forty or fifty years ago, a tree or two, a few large willows near the lakeshore, where there are a couple of expensive places and a few cottages waiting for summer to return. At the point where the river meets the lake, a stone outcropping and a small wharf. In summer, sailboats.

To the north of the main street, the residential streets, a slight slope upward away from the lake, and the lawns green and the trees tall, and most of the houses have a bit of space for a garden. At the top of the slope is the old courthouse, now a township recreational centre. On one of the quiet side streets is the house I used to own. Further west is the place we rented when we first came to town, taller, but less attractive.

If you walk east a block from what was our house, turn right, then left, you will find my current establishment. St Chad's it was when it was in the God business. Now it's the Old Church Theatre, and in the basement – producer, business manager, box office manager, washroom attendant – you find me.

The high school where I taught stands near the highway five miles out of town, built there just before we arrived. Students mostly arrive by bus. I remember the day we came, and how I, a city mouse, walked along the shady streets which I was ready to admit were slow and beautiful, though I wondered if I could learn to be a small-town mouse. Suppose I did.

Trying to shovel the walk at the side door, but a crust of ice has formed on top from the freezing rain that followed the snow, all the trees on the street coated with ice, and toward me, slowly, slowly along the sidewalk creeps a woman in a black coat, with some sort

of metal apparatus on her shoes. Barry Engelhart's great-aunt,
I think she is. We've seen each other around over the years,
but never met. She had no children or grandchildren in the
school.

'Some kind of skates?'

'The very opposite. Little metal teeth to grab the ice and keep
me from falling.'

'Might be safer to stay home.'

'Might be safer to die as well.'

'You only need one fall.'

'I intend to creep once around the block, and I'll do better
without you predicting disaster.'

'You're right. I apologize.'

'I worshipped there,' she says, indicating the stone building
behind me. 'Baptized there. Some time ago now. Must be a cold
place to live.'

'I manage to keep one room warm enough.'

'It would give me the heebie-jeebies.'

'I was never in it when it was a church.'

'Just a building now, I suppose.'

'Where do you go to church now?'

'I go to that United place. Don't think much of it, but it's
convenient, and I don't suppose God makes any distinction. He can
put up with a lot of well-meaning drivel as well as some out-of-
tune chanting. Don't think he cares much what we do one way or
the other. We're the ones who need it.'

'Bert Stoodleigh told me he used to be in the choir here, when
he was a boy.'

'I remember that. Fat little fella.'

'Didn't know him then.'

'It's the communion down at that other place that bothers me
the most, grape juice instead of wine. I don't know that I exactly
believed in transubstantiation or consubstantiation, or whatever I
was supposed to believe in, but the idea of the fermentation, how
sugar turned into alcohol always gave me the idea that one thing
could be another. When I was just a girl I'd imagine that I was

29

drunk on that little sip of wine, and that was holiness, being just a little drunk on God's blood. Hadn't thought of that for years until a few weeks ago. Things come back. I thought of mentioning it to the United Church fella, but I didn't want to upset him. He thinks it's all about being good.'

I've stopped work on the snow and ice, and I am looking at the old face, the eyes still bright blue. I notice that I am standing on the sidewalk on a cold afternoon discussing theology with an old woman with creepers on her shoes.

'Food for thought,' I say.

'Now I haven't heard that phrase for a long time. How old are you?'

'Well, I'm retired.'

'You look too young for that.' She turned away. 'The speed I move I'd better get on my way if I want to be home before dark. Not that there's anyone waiting for me.'

'I know the feeling.'

'So I heard. Well, merry Christmas. Be that soon enough.'

She creeps away.

Meet Busy Bill for coffee: we reflect on the meaning of retirement. His wife wants him to take up a hobby, preferably something that will get him out of the house. I suggest whittling, those duck decoys and other local birds, do bird-watching and go off to craft shows. He says that what he has in mind is a life of crime, but I say the weather is too cold for that. When it gets warm we can have illicit adventures.

I'm surprised when I hear the phone ringing. It rings so seldom, and the jack is upstairs, put in last summer for the box office, and so far away from my little foxhole in the basement that by the time I get there, the caller has usually given up, but today it rings persistently and I stumble upstairs into the bright cold empty church, a wash of wintery sunshine coming through the south windows, and I answer and there is a familiar voice saying 'Merry Christmas'.

'Merry Christmas, Griff. Good of you to call. And thanks for
the shirt.'

'Is anyone there with you?'

'What do you mean?'

'Is anyone there with you?'

'Who would be here with me?'

'That girl.'

'What girl?'

'The one who conned you into buying that place.'

'Why would she be here?'

'The usual reasons a girl is there.'

'You think that Tessa and I have something going?'

'Why else would you be living the way you are?'

'It's for the good of my soul.'

'I was told you were having an affair with one of your old
students.'

'You got that from Barry Engelhart, I suppose. Big wind of the
rumour mill. Lawyer to the elite. Lovely house on the river.
Upright and censorious spouse.'

'Barry's OK.'

'Your old friend Barry is a gossip. How he can combine that
flapping tongue with the discretion that is usually required of a
lawyer to the best families is beyond me.'

'So you're not involved with that girl.'

'Involved?'

'You know what I mean.'

'No, I don't.'

'Of course you do.'

'Tessa has not warmed my bed. If that's what you mean. Not
that I don't have every right, having been abandoned by my wife.'

'You could at least have stayed in the house.'

'I needed a change.'

'I can't understand why you'd do such a thing.'

'Well, I wanted to do it, and I did.'

'Have you been in touch with mother?'

'She sends a postcard now and then. Have you heard from her?'

'A letter.'

'Has she found what she was looking for?'

'I couldn't say.'

'I hope so.'

'I'm sure you encouraged her in this foolishness.'

'Of course. I drove her out so I could indulge my fantasies of raunchy sex with some teenage cream bun.'

'I didn't say that.'

'You implied it.'

'You must admit that you are behaving strangely.'

'Your mother left me. Wouldn't even let me drive her to the airport. So I sold up and started a theatre.'

'Which lost a lot of money.'

'They all do.'

'Don't expect me to keep you.'

'No, I'll go obediently to the workhouse when my hour comes. I've never understood what you do with all your money.'

'Invest it.'

'A careful man.'

'I hope somebody's invited you out for Christmas dinner.'

'Old friends have rallied round. I'm going to Bill's place. He says his wife is a good cook. Old-fashioned I'd expect, but who's to know? Maybe she'll make red and green Christmas sushi. How's Luanne?'

'She's fine.'

'What is she cooking for dinner, turkey or goose?'

'We're going out. There's a hotel here that does a special Christmas dinner. It's very popular. You have to book months ahead.'

'Going out to a hotel?'

'Yes.'

'Tell me, when do I get a grandchild?'

'I'd better go.'

'Good of you to call.'

'Have a nice dinner.'

'Try to keep track of your mother. I'm afraid she's going to die out there.'

* * *

New Year's Eve. Nightmares about the building, the real thing bad
enough. Snow blowing in through the window upstairs, the one I
patched with cardboard and masking tape, and I won't go up the
ladder to repair it because the last time I slipped and nearly fell,
brought down the whole ladder, and besides I no longer have the
ladder, which was borrowed. So I sit here on the corner of a
mattress on the floor of the little church kitchen – stove, fridge,
counter, sink – the duvet pulled around me, a woollen hat on my
head, layers of clothes, gloves, the little electric heater running up
the power bill, both doors of the room closed, and I am warm.

Now and then I wonder where Laura's at, and if it's hot there.
Or is she in the mountains, the place for nirvana, or some equally
spiritual state? Foolish, I thought, but no more so than what I've
done since she left.

Can't see through the frosted glass of the basement window,
real frost over mechanical frosting, but I can hear the wind. Maybe
I'm trapped here, storm-stayed. Across the room the front of the
old stove rests on two copies of the Book of Common Prayer to
keep it level where the floor sags. In the summer I'll get some
chunks of wood to replace them and add them to my small library.
The Oxford Book of Poetry, edited by Sir Arthur Quiller-Couch.
Two torn copies of *National Geographic*. A *Collected Shakespeare*.
A school text of *Madame Bovary*, which I can't read because I don't
know enough French. My tattered copy of *Our Town* – I saved that.
A shelf of other play scripts. *The Portable Graham Greene. A Brief
History of Time*, which I might read if I thought I could understand
it. My paperback text of *Hamlet*. Two historical dictionaries. A
volume of Toynbee. A couple of high school history texts, kept out
of sentimentality since I taught from them for many years.

Tessa could play Hamlet, with butch haircut, nice legs in
tights. Imagine Griff accusing me of doing all this for sex. Not that
I wouldn't, but I didn't.

The wind is blowing, and upstairs there will be little piles of
snow forming below the broken window and inside the ill-fitting
side door.

For breakfast I ate All Bran with the last dribble of two-percent milk. I have some instant coffee and edible oil product to be boiled up later, for warmth and comfort. Will I go down the road to Christy's and shop? Not in this weather. Somewhere far away Laura is sitting on dry mud beneath a tree, the leaves above her all aglitter with hot sun, the branches full of spirit-birds, an endless sky beyond, and a thin brown man is explaining how to avoid explanation, and she spreads her arms in a gesture of acceptance, then brings her hands together in a gesture of prayer. Is her mind pure, or is she wondering what to have for lunch, or if the thin brown man is watching her big breasts – which sag a little now in a way I adore – move with the movement of her arms? Is she wise or only determined to be wise?

There is one kind of wisdom for warm countries, another for the cold – breathe slow, take comfort where you can. Stoicism comes with the climate.

Tessa lives in an apartment in downtown Toronto and gets parts in plays and movies and television and waits to be famous. She is living the life I never lived, the life I abandoned. The city is all movies now. A walk down Yonge Street discovers a camera crew on every street corner. I believe Tessa is touched by greatness. What does that mean? Something. That she can bring the necessary blend of energy and clarity and pain to the chosen souls who sit before her in the dark and live life through her words and acts. She makes them exist more largely for two hours. This is her art. Maybe she should go to London or New York. I could save up my pension cheques and give her the fare.

Maybe she will come battling through the drifted snow, a copy of *The Duchess of Malfi* in the pocket of her parka, one of those parts she's always wanted to play, and the two of us will curl up under the duvet and read it aloud and plan a production for next summer, a few hanging set pieces painted blood-red, ditto the furniture, costumes, everything lit with pure white light. She will ask me to direct her in this production in which she will wear a blood-red body suit with bits of black garment as skirt or regalia. A long purple wrapping for her belly in the pregnant scene. As we

34

plan it, discuss the lines, I will doze off, and in the morning when I wake I will see her on the other side of the mattress, shut eyes under a thicket of eyelashes, breathing slow, bare arm curled against the pillow.

When I am forced to leave this little kitchen-bedroom-parlour to go to the toilet, far off across a bare empty basement, will I have the courage to strip down and wash myself in the middle of this cold and storm? I should have another little electric heater to keep the bathroom warm enough that the pipes don't freeze. The furnace is turned way down to save fuel, and the radiators upstairs turned off. No travellers found on the floor in this weather. The animals are all in hiding.

I hear the wind, listen for the ghost of God.

How was Warren to tell his story, unless he believed it *was* a story, not just *one damned* etc. and he had some difficulty with that. Too young for it, he played Elwood P. Dowd and was charming and vague and funny; still too young, he played George in *Who's Afraid* etc. – and so? Were those moments of *peripeteia?* The school production of *Our Town* he directed, with Tessa Niles as Emily, came to mind as a significant moment, but how to express its meaning; all anyone noticed, he suspected, was his apparent infatuation with the young woman, how he insisted she was the most talented he'd ever met. He was well on in middle age, and she offered him her trust, her ability, and he used it, or she used his, and any observer would point out how possible it was that his assessment of her was, if not wrong, intemperate. Tell him the terrible tales about men running off with their students, and the consuming disaster that came afterward. Who was ever sure if the truth was to be found by a cool detachment or a foolhardy leap? *Tessa is the best ever,* he had said to Laura, and Laura had said, calmly enough, *Or only the prettiest?* In the last scene in the graveyard Tessa managed in some inexplicable way to be in two worlds at once, death and life. After the performance Laura said *Yes, she's good,* and then, *Certainly very, very good.*

Who remembered that play? Warren liked to tell the story of

Patrick Samite, the finest actor of his generation at university, who had become a successful lawyer, his precise, pellucid undergraduate Willy Loman erased. Tessa's performance of Charlotta Ivanovna with her clever conjuring tricks was seen by a few last summer and probably remembered by fewer. Why did anyone give themselves to such futility? Because it used them more fully than anything else in the world. Had anyone ever explained to him the meaning of his story, of all stories, that we want to be used, used up, consumed, our sexual disasters not accidents but a search for oblivion by fire?

Your business is with action alone, not by any means with the fruit of your action.

Night and snow. Snow and night. I lie in bed, planning things. Porridge. Porridge makes for good planning when sleepless at 3 a.m. 'The Scottish Oatmeal Play', written and directed by Warren T. Not for tomorrow morning because I have no oats in my stock of groceries in the little cupboard over the sink, where the church ladies kept this and that, tea and coffee and dry biscuits, to be served at meetings of the sidesmen or wardens, or whoever it is meets in a small Anglican church in a middle-sized town in eastern Ontario. To plan the aforesaid porridge I must arrange an expedition for ingredients. There is, I think, some easy way to make it. Mix and serve. With milk and brown sugar. Do I suppose that Christy's would have such a thing, or will it require a drive to the stripmall with its half-assed supermarket? Or I'll need to go further afield, start up the motor on my (imaginary) motor launch and set off into the grey winter waves of the lake, following the course of the shore until it joins the great river that pours its tons of water each minute down the watercourse that leads to the sea. Everything is far and near.

The next time I awake it is daylight, and my throat feels a little dry and harsh. Unsure whether there was anything worth eating on hand, but when I went to bed it was snowing, and I don't feel much like going out in the cold and snow. People, of course, there were people out there, shovelling the snow, getting cars started, and I could be one of them, sweep snow off the car, slip and slide down the hill and along to Tim's for hot coffee and some sort of breakfast, and then go hunting for oats.

Evening, the radio making soft music as I sit under coats and blankets reading *A Streetcar Named Desire* and wondering if Tessa is old enough to play Blanche. But no one can ever replace Brando as Stanley. This afternoon I stood in the cold church and wondered if we would try again when summer comes back, when the apple trees are covered with blossoms like snow instead of snow like blossoms.

Let's dance, I say to Laura in the dream, and we move together in a style like some version of ballroom dancing. Slippery is the word that comes to me and when I mention it to her, she agrees that our movement is just like that, each taking the signal from the other, where to move and at what speed. We cover vast distances, moving gracefully and at high velocity. It is a skill that we have mastered, but then the air thickens and we are dancing apart, and when I catch glimpses of her in this dim light, she is doing another dance altogether, and I am unable to follow it.

Awake I pull the covers closer around me against the cold of the night, bereft and waiting for dissolution. The dream is still clear, the memory of it precise, though I know by morning it will be forgotten, and I think of it as a defining metaphor for the past when Laura was what she was with me – in our dream dance – and I would have said that the dancer-with-me was what she was, but there was no inevitability to it, and in another life she might have danced otherwise altogether. Is, now. The Laura who was a part of my life has taken French leave, and I have no knowledge of her, who she is, what she has become. The point of jealousy, that our lover is alien when clasped panting in the arms and legs of the other one, enemy. Remember the days when Laura used to exchange letters with a university pal, Alfred Donnelly, who was a professor at McGill. *Alf the Sacred River,* she liked to call him, and now and then she'd quote things he said, enchanted by his way with words, and I never understood this other Laura who was attached to such alien formulations.

I lie in the cold, and the chill has entered my brain or my heart or my soul, whatever part of me creates the trusting continuity of the long years. I am cut off from what I was, that slippery fast dance. I turn on my side and pull the covers over my head, hope to sleep.

Rise early to a winter morning, a light snow and everything blurred by fog. Thought I heard footsteps upstairs, but when I went up, there was no one, just a dim grey foggy light in the empty space that used to be holy. Deconsecrated. Do they have a special service for that? When I get the two copies of the prayerbook out from under the stove I'll have a look. Beyond the church, all the dark winter outlines are inscribed by snow, caressed by mist. My outline is not inscribed by snow. Shave, wonder if the car will start, walk to Christy's for a tin of beans and some wieners, a shaker of cayenne for zing.

Laura is in another country. I hope she had all her shots. Under the great sky Brahman and Atman breathe with a single breath. Every leaf of the tree beneath which she sits is holy. The beggars are holy. The buggers are holy. The hole is holy. The whole is wholly holy. Dear Laura, dear elephant rider, dear elephant arse, don't die. Please don't die.

I wake, and the first thing I am aware of is that I am sick. My body weighs twenty pounds more than it did last night when I went to bed, and my head is two sizes bigger, the brain two sizes smaller. When I try to stand up, I am dizzy, but I gather myself together and stagger to the toilet to empty my bladder. My bones hurt, every single one of them, and there are more of them than you would ever dream. To get up from the toilet seat where I have collapsed demands more energy than my body can summon, but I am beginning to shiver from the cold, so I make the effort, stand and grab hold of the door frame, and step by step make my way back to my den by holding on to the walls. I fill an empty milk carton with water and set it by the head of the bed, swallow the second-last aspirin in the bottle, and then I get myself under the covers, as shivering becomes shuddering which threatens to become shattering, aching bones to fall asunder, and I summon one last bit of determination to reach out for the dressing gown I dropped on the floor and pull it over me on top of the covers, and then I curl myself small and pull all the sheets and blanket closer around me, and over my head, and I prepare myself to die. I am still breathing, each breath an effort. Eyes tightly closed I search for warming thoughts and all that will come is an image of Laura worshipping the sacred phallus of some god or his priest, Smiler grinning as Tessa goes down on him. Why, at the brink of dissolution am I still thinking of women? How to die with dignity? Dignity, there is none, except an illusion, the natural vanity of the young and well, and I am terribly unwell. Shivering has some function in warming us. I read that somewhere. My temperature is rising. Fever. With chills. If only someone would find me, bring more covers, smother me with down comforters, cups of hot honey and lemon. Faces, handsome, serious faces. Shapes. I am trying to dream, but the weight of my body prevents it. If only I could dream I would be asleep and my cells would begin to fight off the sickness that poisons them. One at a time the cells are being devoured by the virus, which nourishes itself on their sweetness, and propagates by a geometrical progression. I must try to stop time and in that way end their subdivision, their automaton war. What I see is little creatures like those in the old Pac-Man games, pure appetite, first gobbling, then invading with a convulsive chemical spread through the invisible fibres. Heaviness. Trying to climb the crooked stairs, and sliding down. Down. I wake suddenly, my skin on fire, and I try to throw back the covers but have no strength. Time slows and then suddenly races, or perhaps it is my heartbeat. I feel sleep close to me and then I am on the same staircase, my feet sliding away from me, and the next time I wake I hear wind rattling the wooden frame of the window, and I reach out and find the carton of water and drink from it, spilling some, but the touch of air chills me, and I start to shiver again. I drink more, in spite of the shivering. Water is my only medicine.

When I open my eyes the room is dark. I imagine that someone is beating on the doors of the church, a search party sent out to find me, but unaware of my helplessness. The telephone upstairs is ringing. Someone is calling with terrible news. It is as well I can't answer, but the ringing goes on and on. When I wake into what seems to be morning it has finally stopped. I drink all the rest of the water, pee into the carton since I know I haven't the strength to get up. I can hear the sound of my breathing, and just as I lapse into unconsciousness I think they are beating on the church door again. In my sleep, if it is sleep, I try to prepare myself for death, and wonder if someone will come to welcome me to Nowhere. The air is a bright whirl of coloured mists, and with my hands I form it into shapes, golden angels of annunciation, bringing the god who will teach me to breathe slowly, evenly, the divine breath that will carry me into non-existence. On the other side of the room, he sits cross-legged, a stone phallus emerging from the bright garments, pointing upward, ringed with flowers, awaiting its worshippers. In a moment it shrivels and vanishes. His face is peaceful, he is uttering meaningless syllables, his hands imitating the movement that mine invented to summon him, performing a kind of slow rocking that is a code for the destruction of the universe, and then he is fading from sight followed by the figures of women in flowing garments. I try to accompany them, but I'm aware that this god is the god of destruction and I am not yet ready for the finality of his realm. I must study for absence.

I lie awake in darkness, thirsty, throat swollen and raw, trying to remember if there is one more aspirin in the bottle. Carefully I get to my feet, holding the counter when the giddiness starts, and when it eases I stand on tiptoe to void my urine into the sink, letting the water run to wash it away, then filling a glass of water and drinking it greedily, slopping a little on the shirt I wear in bed for warmth. In the aspirin bottle there is one more tablet, and I take this as an encouraging sign. Back in bed I shiver, the chills reasserting their authority. I try to remember what day it is, how long I have been sick. I try to envision a goddess of health, to be summoned from the non-world into my veins and nerves, and a half-second of quavering lust encourages me to think that I may survive, but in an instant I am fevered and oblivious once more. Having thought I was better, I feel, more than ever before, the burden of my breathing, a balloon inflated in my chest which makes it almost impossible to continue to take in air, everything quiet except the sound within me of life and death struggling in every tiny blood vessel, every lobe of the lungs, and I am convinced that someone is sitting in the room with me, drawing each breath in the exact rhythm of my breathing, and I give myself to this other, whoever it is, and the effort is less. Almost possible.

I think it is morning again, and the room bright with sunlight. I am still alive. Am I getting better? Maybe. Remember a favourite old story, and I almost laugh. But I am not ready to stand. Even the thought of it is too much, and after a few quiet minutes the death machine starts up again, dizziness, a whining in my ears, the same struggle to breathe and I dive into my bones and hide there, wake in the dark, cry out weakly for help, mostly to see if my voice still works, and but the confusion of drums in my ear blots out the possible voices. Everything is damp, and I wonder if I have wet the bed, conclude that it is sweat pouring off me, and the next time I see daylight, I am parched and burning, and I force myself to stand, pour water into myself and lie down again. Now I lie awake staring at the ceiling. The light is grey and thin, early morning or late afternoon, no sun, the dim reaches of winter, snowing perhaps. I lie there for a long time, but I am awake and cool and transparent, a little better now, and I think I might eat something. If I had the strength to rise. Without food I will not gain the strength to stand up and get the food. I feel that I am confronting some deep philosophical conundrum – freedom and necessity, one of those large puzzles that take a lot of cogitation to wrestle down.

Slowly, limb by limb, I extract myself from the bed, and try to find nourishment. A spoonful of marmalade, straight from the jar. Another and then some All Bran chewed down dry, and from the refrigerator, just behind my tax returns, an apple, soft and about to rot but edible and I eat it. I piss in the sink, rinse it down, fill a glass of water. Back in bed I rest for a while, working on a plan to boil water and mix up instant coffee with sugar and an edible oil product and drink it scalding hot. I believe that the telephone is ringing upstairs, but it is too far. The North Pole would be as likely a destination.

Interior. Tim Hortons. Day.

'You look awful,' Bert says.

'That's why I'm drinking this double-double and eating two cream-filled doughnuts. They'll give me strength.'

'You must have been pretty rocky.'

'There was one time I thought I was dead. It got very quiet and the shivering stopped.'

'You should have called someone.'

'I couldn't get to the phone. All I could do was lie there. I kept drinking water when I could stand up and get to the sink. I figure that's what saved me – all the chemicals they put in it.'

'But you're OK now?'

'Yesterday I washed myself, turned up the thermostat and called down for pizza. Billy doesn't usually deliver, but I told him I was sick and I hadn't eaten for days. So he made me a vegetarian special and got some kid who hangs around there to drive it up. You know what tasted good? The onions. And all that salty cheese.'

'You shouldn't be there all by yourself.'

'Lots of people live alone.'

'Some have more talent for it.'

'What does that mean?'

'I'm not sure, but it's true.'

'You're getting all philosophical.'

'I guess.'

'When I was sick I remembered a story I once heard.'

'And?'

'Well, there was this old fella lived by a border between two countries. And he'd ride his donkey back and forth on business, trading, you know, buying and selling. Now the customs man knew

he was smuggling, but he could never catch him. Never. Well, years
later they're retired, both of them, and one day the customs man
meets the fella, and he says that maybe now he can tell him what
he was smuggling. "Donkeys," he says.'

'... and ...'

'That's it.'

'I think maybe I'm missing something here.'

'Never mind. Some people think it's a little bit deep.'

'I thought maybe it was supposed to be funny.'

'That too.'

'So you remembered that when you were sick.'

'You want another coffee? My treat.'

'I better get back to work. Listen, you come to dinner tonight.
June will make you some real food. You're so pale I could probably
see your bones.'

'When's her birthday?'

'October.'

'Then why did they call her June?'

'Just high spirits, I guess.'

I want that Book of Common Prayer, one of them, but I don't have
the strength or wit to get it out from under the stove. I want to
know how you deconsecrate something. Officially. Not just let it go
and forget about it. If I once learned that, I could go around the
world deconsecrating things. Officially. As it is everything is pretty
well deconsecrated anyway, but it would be nice to see the
paperwork completed.

Then there's the Chekhov. When the phone rang this morning I
managed to get to it in time to answer, and it was Dick Burkwitz
from the community college. They're having a conference on
Funding the Arts, and he was looking for a little one-man show,
and I said *On the Harmfulness of Tobacco* would be about right,
maybe fifteen minutes, funny if I get it right, and Dick said,
Sounds great, and gave me a date, time and place, which I wrote
on the back of my hand, lacking a piece of paper. As I did I
realized I was a little confused about just what the date is today,

lost track when I was sick and never quite caught up. So the first thing I have to do is find a calendar or a date book – maybe something at the drug store – and the second thing I have to do is find a script of that little monologue. Had one – all Chekhov's one-act pieces – but didn't keep it, of course. It went in the general disburdening, and now I'll have to pay good money for something I owned a year ago. And where to find it?

Imagine, I have work to do, a part to play.

The elephant postcard that Laura sent sits on the table, propped against the shaker of cayenne. Yes, I now have a table, and the remains of a chair. When I had dinner with Tubby Bert, June, his handsome wife, asked me about furniture, and I said that I didn't have a lot, and she said there was a little table she was trying to get rid of, and suddenly acquisitive, I said, I'll take it, and I remembered that in the closet behind the Sunday school room here there was a broken chair, and with a bit of string I repaired it, so now I can sit at the table and stare at the elephant and wait for elephant wisdom to arrive.

I phoned around and a text of the Chekhov play is in the mail. I last played it many years ago when I was maybe too young for the part. You're always too young for the part or too old for the part. *Make yourself up and pretend – it's called acting:* what old St John Masters used to say. Make them look at the rope and believe it's a serpent. And who's to say the rope is real anyway. Personality is what we perform when we think we're not performing.

The days are growing perhaps a jot or a tittle longer, but there's no end to the wind and storm. Windows rattling again. It has been snowing all day. I wonder what I would do if the power went off. Tramp up the stairs and recite as much as I recall of Lear on the heath, then climb into bed, I suppose, with every blanket and garment in the building on top of me and wait for the electricity to come back. In the closet beneath the broken chair I found some maroon velvet curtains, which are now my bedspread, heavy as all

44

get out. I wish I could see through the windows of this room. Damn frosted glass. If I want to observe the dangerous height of the drifts I have to peer out one of the side windows of the Sunday school or, once they're covered, climb the stairs to peek out the little window in the side door. I should have stocked up on tins of things to eat. I have onions, bought because I enjoyed them on that life-saving pizza, a couple of tins of soup, one tin of beans and some wieners in the frosty little freezer compartment in the corner of the ancient refrigerator. Creative cooking: mix them all together in a pot with a few shakes of cayenne. It's possible that I should cook and eat something now while the scurrying electrons are still reaching as far as the old church stove.

If I had my copy of the Chekhov playlet I could run lines. Instead I sit on the mattress, a glass of wine in my hand, back against the wall, blankets round me, listening to the increasing power of the wind, hoping the lights don't fail, and I read *The Third Man* for the Fourth Time. Never meant to be published, Greene says, blah, blah, blah, but I don't have the film at hand, only this Ur-text, and as the dark closes in, I hear a pounding at the church door. Knock. Knock. Knock. The drunken porter at the gate of hell welcoming the arrivals to their damnation. Knock. Knock. Knock. It's deconsecrated here, solitary, hell enough, and by the time I have scrambled up the stairs across the dark church to open the door, the messenger will have departed into the tempest.

Open the west door and in blows a bushel of blizzard, the wind seizing the door, dragging me with it, cold penetrating my clothing, and in the dark and dangerous afternoon, behold a tall figure on skis and covered in scarves, hats, snow, maybe speaking, but in the wind-screech I can't hear a word. Signal this ghost to enter, and find a light switch that turns on a little bulb in the vestibule, and in clomps she (it appears from the slender shape to be a female ghost), skis and all, and I pull the door closed, against the drag of the wind, a near thing not to be hauled out and whisked away. The face wrapped in a long scarf is unwrapped, and proves to be young and pink-cheeked with the storm, and familiar, yes, Mara Paulsen, recently returned to be music teacher for all the primary schools of the township.

She asks whether I am OK, and I assure her that I am indeed OK, though a little apprehensive about the power going off, and she says that the internet says that the storm will last all night, and we both babble and it emerges that she has a message from Tessa, who has been phoning me but I never answer. Well, I was sick. Perhaps I've gone deaf. So Tessa called Mara, old school friend, and asked for a message to be delivered by Great Dane, and it appears that Mara in her own strapping person is the required Great Dane, and as she skied over, she was convinced I'd be found dead. I beat my chest to prove myself alive, then promise to call Tessa, and make Mara my best offer of hospitality, beans and wieners with red wine, onions and lots of cayenne, but it appears she would rather go back out into the storm than risk that gourmet delight. Door, wind, blizzard, Warren nearly whirled away again, the door tugged to with both arms, the old iron catch caught, and I stumble back downstairs to warm myself in my cavern, call Tessa later.

Curled up in bed in the dark of night, I shiver, and for a moment wonder if the illness, malady infection, fever, flu, grippe, consumption, is about to make a return. Imagine tropical warmth, Laura under her magic tree, and the fantasy turns on itself, and now the picture is of Laura in our bathroom, seated on the fluffy toilet seat, naked as a jaybird (explain that old saying – can't), bent over her big round jugs, the right one resting on a lifted knee, as, foot in hand, she cuts her toenails, click, click, click, carefully putting the clippings into the soil of the Boston fern that sits on a wicker stand close to the window, which is hung with a curtain of white cotton that filters the bright summer sunlight.

Who will cherish this memory when I am gone? Wisest and best to leave no trace. What comes to me is not wisdom but only such vivid particularities, how her breast was crushed against her knee, my concern about whether toenails are good for Boston ferns.

46

The car won't start. This is a serious matter, as I am due in Toronto this afternoon. About a job. A part in a TV series – three appearances, one in each episode of a three-part miniseries. I use that word so easily. Miniseries. When last I appeared on television, that word didn't exist. Probably the whole conception didn't exist. You did a television play. A drama. Live. I can remember when television was mostly live, and the most astonishing disasters occurred. By the time I quit they'd started shooting to tape and editing.

Don't get wrapped up in the past, Warren, the car, which is to carry you to your new future, won't start and you have no other way of getting to the audition. Call the garage on the highway a few miles away and hope that they will come promptly, jump-start the car or tow it in and repair it in a brisk fifteen minutes, and somehow get you to the big city on time for this unlikely audition, which you owe to the lovely and talented Miss Tessa Niles, who has a big part in the same miniseries and suggested you to the casting director and to her own agent, who will negotiate the contract if you should happen to get cast, and you will have to get Tessa to teach you how they make TV in these modern days so you don't look like a fool. She did, will do, all this, not just because she believes in your great talent, but because she feels she owes you money over last summer, and I gather from our chat on the phone, she wants to do it again this summer, and it's time she made, in however roundabout a fashion, a financial contribution. So get the car started and get the part.

A: No, the car didn't go. B: Yes, I got the part.

Another former student saved my bacon. Lighting crew. Hanging and plugging Fresnels in unlikely places, one arm round the bar, toes on the top of the ladder, and it was my job to make them do it safely, but instead I just let them be, and it all got done. They approved. Name of Bernie Boccaloni, now driver of the tow truck for his uncle's garage. Towed me in and heard the verdict, engine full of snow, might take hours or days to dry it out, and when I wept and howled he rented me his car for twenty bucks and I'd fill the tank when I got back – big tank, he warned me. Still, it got me to Toronto in time, and I read for the casting agent and she made me an appointment to read for the director a couple of hours later, and the director listened to me, asked me to read one line differently, then nodded at the casting agent. Said I was funny, and I gathered that was what was required. I called Tessa who wasn't home and left a message on her machine to say I got the part, *merci beaucoup,* and I gathered we had a scene together so I'd be seeing her, and I met with Tessa's agent who was negotiating for me and is now putting me on her list, as a client, impressed that I knocked off the audition and that I'd kept up my union membership, out of some kind of superstition mostly, and now I am back in my hole in the ground, and they will deliver my car when they get it dried out.

Oh yes. The director said he liked the way I'd dressed for the audition. Eccentric, just right for the part. I didn't tell him I always dress this way. Maybe when the car comes back I should motor over to the hardware place and buy a cheapo mirror. Also a thirty-meter extension cord for the phone so I can set it on the stairway close enough to hear and answer. They will call with my shooting schedule. Imagine me having a shooting schedule. It was all so easy. Because I didn't need it, I suppose.

In the forest schools the acolytes listen to fables of the animals, how the lion learned from the monkey, the elephant from the serpent. There is always wisdom to be found if you can remember the right fable. I once played Lion in an entertainment for children, and when I was concealed in the animal suit, the animal head covering my own, my limbs were quick to learn new movements. Feline, lethal. I discovered delight in vanishing into the universe of the beasts.

Once upon a time the elephant came to the edge of the jungle, and in the jungle it was very dark. He wondered how he could find his way in the dark. But in a tall tree above him he saw a monkey,

and spoke to him. Tell me, how can I find my way through the
dark jungle? the elephant said. By staying in the treetops, close to
the sky, the monkey said.
And what did Big Ears say to that?

Lift the lid of the trunk that contains all my secrets. Well, not
exactly. What it contains is a heap of this and that, tossed in as I
teetered on the edge of a new world the night before the auction.
Anything I didn't want sold off went either into garbage bags to be
hauled away or into this trunk, and I hardly remember now which
sentimental souvenir went in which place. Tossed out Laura's
remaining clothes, wept a little as if disposing of the knickers of
the dear departed. Was. And the woollies she had put on three
layers thick to set off cross-country skiing in our winter sport
period.

In one corner at the bottom of the trunk I observe the small
metal container that contains my mother's ashes. One of my
failures, to find an appropriate place to dispose of them. She was,
after all, my mother, and somewhere in here is a framed picture of
the two of us in a rowboat on an imaginary river somewhere far off
in my childhood, and we are both smiling. You can't just dump the
scorched remains in the garbage. Besides it's probably illegal.
Nearly everything is. But while I didn't want to toss them carelessly
aside, I had in later years lost track of her, somehow, of what she
most cared about. Spread them over a place where she was happy.
Mostly she wasn't especially happy, and the house in East York
with a little garden she liked was long gone. I suppose the ashes
will come to no harm here in the trunk. Maybe next summer I'll
take them down to the river with me and set them adrift. It's quiet
down there. She liked quiet. Laura used to trip over the box in the
closet now and then, and she would bawl me out for my
sentimentality or indecisiveness or whatever she thought my failing
was that day, and I would snap back that she had disposed of her
parents so efficaciously because she had no soul. And she in turn
would fire back that I didn't have more soul, but only less brain.
Lucky she doesn't know that lying on top of the box of ashes,

wrapped in tissue paper, are her baby photographs, a crocheted shawl made by her great-grandmother, and her silver christening cup. Was I to send them to the landfill?

Upright, tightly pressed against the side of the trunk stand two or three picture frames. A drawing of Laura at eighteen, nude, before I ever met her, done by an art student she fancied. A gentle sort of drawing, a kind of silhouette against a window. James, the art student in question, later came out of the closet, gave up art and, if Laura is to be believed, became an undertaker. Should hang it up. Later.

In front of naked Laura there's a picture that I clipped out of a magazine and put in a second-hand frame that happened to fit. The photograph shows Matisse in his old age, fat, bald, barefoot, sitting in a wheelchair, in his fingers a pair of scissors and all around him on the floor, bits of paper from the collage pieces he is cutting out. Against the wall the shapes of a huge collage called *La Négresse*. Something about the colossal kindergarten play of his last years made me clip out the photo and save it. He was over eighty, dying slowly of bowel cancer, but from his bed or his chair he kept on drawing, cutting, pasting. I should live so long and die so brilliantly – I suppose that's what I thought.

The next little frame contains a review of my performance in *Look Back in Anger*. A review by Nathan Cohen, and he said good things about me. Rare for him to like anything, that Cape Breton curmudgeon. I thought after that I would have a career. Now I'm starting over, I should hang it over my mattress for encouragement; a historic document. I used to spend two weeks in the fall in my senior history course talking about the nature of historic documentation. What is a fact? Well, that frame holds a fact of sorts.

In front of the frames I stuffed a little album of pictures from my first year of summer stock, the year before Laura turned up, pictures of me with Daisy. An older woman. Dizzy Daisy. But she was kind to me, taught me a thing or two. No hell as an actress, but she had a generous spirit and a soft heart. She told me that if I wanted a career I should move to New York or London, and in those days that was probably true, but I hung around Toronto, met Laura etc., etc. Now and then in the dark of night I have wondered if I knew that I was set to choose between Art and Sex and was going for the fluffy bed in the soft hotel. True? Laura might have followed me into a gypsy life if I'd asked her. Didn't. Too broke. Doing it now.

On top of the frames and the album lies a box that once contained a blouse, now full of souvenirs and clippings from my years of productions at the high school, Tessa in *Our Town* and the talented Bobby MacDonald in *Teach Me How to Cry*, and a cast of thousands in various musicals. Hey, Mr Thouless, can we do *Grease*, can we do *The Sound of Music*, can we do *Li'l Abner*? We did them all.

In another corner, rolled up in a cardboard tube to keep it safe, is the batik hanging that Laura and I bought at a craft show at the community college, jungle colours, bright flowers and exotic birds, and she put it on the wall behind the carpet where she did yoga. I could unroll it and install it on the wall somewhere, but in these big rooms I suppose it would be lost. Perhaps at the front of the church, where a cross might have hung, this pantheist icon. To go with that polychrome blaze of growth, I would, if I could procure any such thing, install a panel of erotic carvings from a temple of Shiva. A book of them once passed through our hands, borrowed from someone. 'Holy fuck,' I said as I flipped the pages. Laura laughed.

Lying on top of Laura's baby things I see a chapbook of poems by my college friend Dieter Schmidt, who became a professor of Roman history at Stanford. And beside it, tied up with string, letters he sent in the early years, full of deep speculations on the nature of history and the meaning of Latin inscriptions. I have no letters from Laura because we were never apart long enough. A small square cardboard box holds cufflinks I never wear and my father's pocket watch, which doesn't work. He was growing old and running down, and the watch ran down, and then time stopped.

A dried corsage lies in another small box, which once held Laura Secord chocolates. It was among Laura's things, and I kept it because it was inexplicable. With it was a Chinese fortune saying *Everything goes frequent for you.*

Wedding certificate. Graduation certificates given to Laura and me to prove we were educated. A tie clip my mother gave me when I was eighteen. A shin plaster signed by both my parents when they were young lovers, and in the envelope with it an old Montreal transit ticket. A piece of decorative embroidery done by some member of Laura's family. Griff's favourite jigsaw puzzle, two pieces missing. His teddy bear. Why do I keep these things? I am not, I would have said, a sentimental man, but I couldn't just toss them in a plastic bag and send them away.

Buried somewhere, in an envelope with a printed return address from my father's real estate office, the obituary of my older brother Thomas Clifford Thouless. Crib death, before I was born. My father said that my mother never got over it. I was, I came to believe, merely a shadow of the lost son. No wonder I wanted to act. To be real as someone else, not being real as myself. This is a story I don't tell.

And. And. And.

Close the trunk.

Tomorrow is my first day of shooting. The car will start, at least it chugged agreeably when I tried it tonight, and I will be up at 6:00 a.m. and on my way, coffee and doughnuts from Tim's to be eaten on the 401, and I should be there at least an hour and a half before my call. All my scenes are to be shot in studio, so I expect them to be on time. Two scenes today. There's been a break in the weather this week, warm, dry days, and the radio tells me the roads will be bare. I intend to drive back after the shooting is over, return on Tuesday for the last scene, the one with Tessa.

I lie on my mattress, not sleeping, look for some harmless intoxicating fantasy to lead me away, but I find I'm running the few lines I have to deliver, doing bizarre alternate readings, trying to remind myself not to act in front of the camera, counting the years since I did television, and at last decide to run lines from the Chekhov playlet and maybe I'll doze off.

52

Next thing I know I'm driving down the Don Valley and it feels like ten minutes later that I'm driving out again, trying to look back through the day, think about what I did and said, and whether the performance was acceptable. What if I'm awful? Warren's Last Stand left on the cutting room floor.

Sunday morning the sun is shining when I wake, and I walk downtown and go to Tim's for breakfast. Various old guys on site. They rumble and guffaw over local matters, and as I pass by on my way for a second coffee and a doughnut to wash down the cheese biscuit I've devoured, one of them – used to drive truck for the township but I can't remember his name – nods to me, and on the way back he catches my eye and says, Are you starting a new religion up in the church there? And I say, Well, maybe, but I haven't quite got it figured out yet. Well, when you do, he says, I'm willing to preach, and his pals find that a pretty funny one, and one of them starts about the TV evangelists his wife supports.

I sit back down and dunk my doughnut in my coffee and try to imagine the tenets of a new religion that I could start. Outside the window the sun is shining, and I recall that the Sun God did a pretty good business in Egypt in past millennia. Maybe I could start a new cult of the sun. But it's already underway when you think of it, all those winter trips to Florida or the Dominican, bikinis on the beach and old fat guys giving them the lecher's look and wearing funny hats because the sun is dangerous now, skin cancer just one more way to go, so maybe the Sun God is not quite right, and besides, while it's a decent enough day, it's still pretty crisp on the ears. Just as I get back to my church I see the elderly woman in the black coat coming along, so I wait and say hello. No creepers on her feet today, pavements bare.

'Can I look inside?' she says.

'Why not?'

So we go up to the side door. I've kept the little sidewalk shovelled. I unlock the door and stand aside for her to go in.

'You first,' she says, so I go first, stand there and wait while she enters, slowly, apprehensive, as if the godlessness of it might strike

53

her down. She looks around her, everything bare, the room empty except for a pile of the risers from last summer in the back corner. Turns to the front where the altar once stood, looking as if it's all she can do not to genuflect.

'Some people might be comfortable with it,' she says.

'But you aren't.'

She just shakes her head. I'm glad I didn't hang up my jungle batik at the front. I expect it would have upset her. The sun is shining in the south windows, and there is a patch of brightness on the floor, curving to a point in the way the windows do. She is staring at it, the Sun God making his clear but complicated statement. She turns and walks back toward the door.

'Too much emptiness,' she says.

At the doorway she turns and looks back at me, her black coat a sharp outline against the banks of snow beyond.

'I get a ride to the United with the couple down at the corner.'

She draws the door shut behind her and sets off through the empty streets. I think of old women wandering the streets alone and remember the out-of-date copy of the *National Post* I found lying beside my chair as I was waiting to shoot my scenes. Once every week they list the crimes that have taken place in Toronto, all the robberies, assaults, sexual attacks. Toronto's a big city, and most weeks they can find quite a few crimes to put on the list. Helps keep people frightened as they go about their depleted and homely lives. Most of us have something to fear and resent, and the list of crimes keeps the irritation raw. A fearful population is easily worked. Sez I.

Good stuff we got on Friday, the director says on Tuesday morning as he blocks my scene with Tessa. Last night he saw the rushes. I'm relieved. We run the scene, once and again with camera, it goes well for both of us, a couple of angles, key closeup of Ms Niles, though I figure my performance is still only halfway there when the director shouts, Cut, print, and we're finished. Over. Time to go home. Instead of immediately setting off into the country, Tessa says, I must meet her for dinner. Have a talk about the summer.

She has another couple of scenes to shoot, so I drive from the studio to a parking lot on Spadina and pass the time in second-hand bookstores, looking at copies of books I once owned, and later we meet in a dark restaurant on Queen Street, and we drink a little and eat a little, and the streetcars, lit like spaceships, pass by in the night. After a while we discuss the summer, and she announces that this time we have to make some money. She has her eye on a clotheshorse who writes about the arts for one of the newspapers, and she plans to strip off his stylish threads and extract a promise of a story on the second season in the old church. I am thinking that I prefer not to know who she's going to undress when she begins to announce her plans for me. We'll do *Our Town*, she says, and bring in audiences. She's a little old for Emily now, I'm about to suggest, when she makes clear that she, Tessa, plans to direct the play, maybe cast the kids locally, and I, Warren, now rediscovered as a performer, am to play the Stage Manager. I look at the thick eyelashes, the white teeth and the straight nose, and I think what a lovely idea to have Tessa ordering me around on stage. Then suddenly there is a lot of shouting, and a couple of people from this afternoon's crew join us, and gossip flows like wine and wine flows like gossip, until I mention to Tessa that I'd better get a hotel room, since I am beyond driving home. Stay with me, she says, I have room. Leave your car in the lot overnight. Sobered by the thought I switch to coffee, and stare out the window at the blue-lit interiors of the spaceships, all those strangers passing by from one unreality to another.

The continuity girl, who is fifty and handsome and a little hard-bitten, is astonished that I am Tessa's old high-school teacher, though I can't make out quite why. She is so astonished that she gets up and leaves, and soon enough we are all leaving, and in the taxi, Tessa leans over and kisses me on the cheek. I tell her not to feed the animals, and she laughs.

Her apartment is near the mental hospital, further out Queen, at the corner another bar, which she says is her local, but she doesn't like the band that's playing tonight. As we walk up the stairs I feel a little dizzy, grasp the banister more firmly. The apartment itself is nondescript, not unpleasant, and while I am in the bathroom, she puts a pillow and a couple of blankets on the couch in the living room. Doors lead off to her bedroom, the kitchen, the loo. She asks if the couch will be OK. I say it will. I am such an agreeable fella. Off she goes, I extinguish the lamp, take off some clothes and lie down. I feel a little dizzy again.

Outside in the street, I hear a car engine racing, a door slams, wheels burn rubber. From the bar at the corner I can hear the sound of the rock band Tessa doesn't like, but muted by walls and distance. I hear the sound of her bare feet coming from the bedroom. In the almost darkness, dim light from the window, I can make out the figure of Tessa padding to the bathroom, the pale loveliness of long bare legs, a long sweatshirt perhaps not quite covering the rest, and she goes into the bathroom, light under the door, and water runs, a toilet flushes, the door opens again and I stare across the darkened room, and she says, *Goodnight, Warren,* and the bare feet cross the floor to her bedroom. She doesn't close the door, and I wonder about the significance of that. Am I invited to join her? Tessa is blunt. If she wanted me she would have said so, though I'm certain that if I got up and stumbled across the dim room to her bed, she wouldn't scream. She is a generous, straightforward person, and she would let me climb in with her. Let me. And I would lie there hoping not to snore obnoxiously, fart egregiously. I have got through the day without being a fool. More than once I made her laugh. As I consider my situation and whether kindliness is enough I realize that while I am imagining Tessa naked in my arms I am half asleep, and I let my somnolence have its way. In the night I am awake for a moment and I hear the siren of an ambulance, as if it carried off some victim of the weird dissections of my dreams.

In the morning I wake to hear someone singing quietly, and when I open my eyes I see that she is still wearing the same shirt but has pulled on a pair of track pants and is making coffee. After a cup she'll set off to the gym where she works out. Then home for a shower and off to the studio where she shoots her next scenes early this afternoon. I drink half a cup of coffee, and as I prepare to leave, Tessa puts her hand on my shoulder and kisses me lightly on the lips, and I go quickly, since I think I might cry.

Walking down to Queen Street I feel that the universe is about to spring out and maul me with its sharpness. Near the corner on the side wall of a grocery store someone has been stencilling, ZEUS, ZEUS, ZEUS, twelve times, evoking that lapsed deity to bring him back to the world of his athletic amours with pretty mortals, one perhaps imminent as the sky father observed a passing maiden with a plump lower lip and spatulate fingers. Beneath the four-letter name, another scribbled in Greek characters. And the rest of the wall is covered with the loose curves of graffiti, the colourful and fluent draughtsmanship of the spray can, swooping and swirling patterns of yellow, orange, red: the movement of the eye following them induces vertigo.

The air is chilly, but the sky is clear and the morning sun catches everything at a low angle, the textures in sharp relief. Mine eyes dazzle. I am pregnant with new meanings, big-bellied, and I waddle round the corner, draw open the glass door of a restaurant, a long narrow space with booths and a counter, behind it the cook in his apron, a big man but pallid, thinning grey hair. Strong coffee, and the cheerful waitress takes my order for eggs over easy with crisp bacon and home fries, and behind the counter, the cook shifts himself between the grill, where he spreads slices of bacon, and the burners, where he dribbles oil into the curved bowl of his egg pan, and heats the pan and cracks two eggs into it, and after a minute of sizzle, he flips the eggs into the air and catches them on the other side, a little magician's trick offered to me with my breakfast, and even as I eat I keep an eye out to see if he will repeat the skillful little flip, and he does.

The pavement, as I walk to the streetcar stop, is full of beggars and angels. Entering the Queen car, going east to the parking lot where I have left my own vehicle – a fortune to be paid for overnight parking – I notice a young woman with wide dark eyes staring out the window, and on her rounded forehead a black smudge of dirt. Almost prepared to call her attention to it, being helpful, when I realize that it's the mark of ashes. This must be the first day of Lent, and she has risen early for the imposition of ashes on her very young and very pretty face. She has climbed from her solitary bed, tossed aside the white cotton nightgown, dashed into the shower and out, then knelt in the cool fragrant darkness of a small brick church on a side street, and the priest has drawn the sign of the cross on her skin.

I sit and watch all the faces that pass, the streets where the crimes to be collected this week by the *National Post* will soon occur, and I study the straight black hair on the head of the girl marked with ashes, as if she might be my accidental daughter, and for a moment I am breathless. I have climbed a tall mountain and am surveying the limits of the world. The streets of the city are crowded, full of beings being, and I was born here, but this was never our part of town, we lived in the east end, and I look down from the mountain and see the three of us, my mother in her blue hat with purple violets and my father in his grey fedora, walking along the Danforth to a restaurant for dinner to celebrate my mother's birthday.

Next summer on a night of the full moon I will invite Tessa to share my mattress on the floor of the deconsecrated kitchen.

Imagine God (or Dionysus or Kali) surveying the empty church on a cloudy afternoon as one man of middling height, Warren Thouless, book in hand, stood alone in the large empty space of his deconsecrated temple rehearsing Chekhov's little lecture, *On the Harmfulness of Tobacco*. From time to time he stopped to make notes on a photocopy of the text – revising the anonymous translation. He had searched the book thoroughly, but it offered not the slightest hint of who might be responsible for the English text, and since it was, in every sense, unspeakable, he felt free to rewrite it. The lecturer, as he impersonates him, wobbling a little, uncertain just how and how much to move, takes a quick glance offstage to see if his wife is observing him, struggles to deliver the lecture she has set up for him, but is unable to resist wandering off into the tales of his befuddled life, daughters, jobs in his wife's boarding school for girls. Warren, as he spoke and revised and spoke again, looking to the book then away, was trying to decide just how funny this was supposed to be, whether to play it altogether for laughs or to attempt something subtler. What he must do was imagine an audience, guess at how a room full of strangers would respond to his little tricks.

He worked for close to an hour, then sat on the edge of one of the platforms piled against the wall and closed his eyes, weary. As he sat there he was contemplating prudence, trying to imagine a life altogether without the pedestrian virtue. Once he had planned to teach a unit on the history of prudence to his senior class, but he had abandoned the idea. What he had wished to set before them was the connection he perceived between the idea of history, the making of plans, and the prudential motive. Himself, he had now abandoned prudence as an approach to living. Or was that only a failed intention, like all other failed intentions? A wise and objective observer, the imaginary God, seeing all, might conclude that for all his gestures he had changed little in his new life, a few outward circumstances altered, and that, like all humans, he was incapable of true freedom. The unimaginable. A being without limits cannot compete in a race, Warren had read somewhere. Gods cannot count.

A call from my agent. The phrase makes me laugh. An audition next week for a commercial. Good money in them, she says. What will I advise people to buy? Beer? Cars? A cure for baldness? Viagra?

I am standing crazed and stunned and naked in the cold space of the old church, as the first light arrives in the sky – a little earlier every day now, the earth each hour spinning at a different angle to the fireball that grants us the grace of existence, minutes creeping toward the equinox. The space around me is haunted by the half light, haunted too by the emptiness that surrounds you when you listen for noises that don't occur and yet batter the body with their non-existence. Last night I drank much wine, and then how easy to dance in the darkness here, ardent and ungainly, seeking death and its opposite in each jerk of the knees and elbows, privities flopping, until breathless I made my way down the stairs in the darkness, almost fell, crawled into the den of sheets and blankets and awaited metamorphosis. Depletion and paralysis as I attended something vast, unlimited, which would encompass and invade, and nothing came. If I spoke out loud I knew the words would be lost. On the edge of sleep a voice cried out to me, from far off. This, I understood, was the peculiar sonority of telepathic communication, though I had never heard it before. It was Laura's voice, wordless yet explicit, calling from a mountain where the divine minions were coming for her, to tear her body to bits, and I listened to the sound and tried to answer it, not aloud, not in explicit syllables, but in the way of its own arrival. Just as I was about to reach her, to set up contact over the curve of the world, spirit bouncing from satellite to satellite and coming down on her like rain, I lost consciousness.

This morning I woke at dawn and dragged myself out of the covers to climb the stairs into the church, impelled to it as if I had left something behind, my soul, my double, and now I wait in despair for it to return to me, look down at the naked body with its lumps and spots and bruises and hairs and appendages. I listen for the return of the telepathic voice, but silence echoes off the stone and about my head. Laura no longer cries out to me. The minions have run her down. She is gone. No, unbearable.

By the side door a couple of pizza boxes for recycling, a green garbage bag full of the detritus of my life. I imagine climbing into a large size plastic bag, sealing the top and putting myself out for collection. Death by compaction, or perhaps if the seal is tight I would already have asphyxiated, joining my lost brother Thomas in the universe of the unbreathing.

In the middle of the room I look toward the vanished altar. The bare wall where I will one day hang the batik, pantheist emblem of the One that is all of the Many. When Smiler was staging *The Cherry Orchard* last summer we couldn't afford either the time or money to build a false wall and provide a crossover and wings, so he moved the playing area forward, and the six feet close to the wall was left dark enough that one could only see the shadows of the actors who waited there for their entrances, sitting on straight chairs as still as the figures of the dead in *Our Town*. The action was haunted by these dim ghosts offstage. As the life Chekhovian is haunted.

I sit naked on the cold wooden floor, legs crossed as best I can and I hold my spine upright and breathe slowly and imagine I am joining Laura in her acts of contemplation, bringing her back to life by the force of my imitation. I will keep this up until the shivering grows too much for me.

I didn't get hired for the commercial, but I have the nice cheque for my TV gig. Pay off my bills. Please Bert by taking care of the back taxes. The agent promises an audition for an American flick that is shooting next month.

Tomorrow is my performance of the Chekhov. I have been busy at the photocopy shop and my character has a little bundle of lecture notes which offer me a prompt script. Yesterday I drove to Wimpy's Clothing Barn on the highway a half hour away and procured a costume, lucky enough to discover an out-of-date swallowtail coat a size too big and some black trousers with a white shirt and black bow tie. Not exactly nineteenth-century Russian, but old-fashioned and strange enough. In a burst of theatrical vanity I bought a cheap mirror from Canadian Tire and dressed myself up for it. Not bad. I will put some butter in my remaining hair and brush it into erection. It's my belief that the college has a gym and showers where I can wash out the butter afterward. If not I can fry my head for dinner.

Outside it is snowing, winter having one last tantrum. I hope the car will start.

Well, that was an adventure. Dried once during the performance, not surprising, old and out of practice, but had my cues in large type there on the lectern as I passed back and forth, looking for, fleeing from, my offstage waiting wife, gave myself a prompt and set forward again. The audience seemed to be laughing quite a lot. Yes, I was thinking, this is a job done well enough. *Dixi et animam levavi.* I delivered the Latin tag, bowed and walked off, as the stage directions bade me do, and since they were applauding heartily, I returned and bowed again and went off again, except that the room had no backstage, so I went out the door and once the applause died down, returned to pick up my belongings, stowed in a corner in a club bag I used to take to the curling rink. One or two of those leaving the room nodded and smiled, badges on their chests to remind them who they were and what conference they were attending this week, and suddenly a woman of a certain age confronted me. I had seen her sitting in the front row, flyaway hair dyed bright orange, a smile on the purple stain of her broadly painted lips, a poor match for the hair, sitting up straight in her chair, almost as tall sitting, I noticed now, as she was standing. Short legs, thick from the waist down, heavy maquillage, those mauve lips smeared on the white face, tangerine eyebrows, a forbidding figure all in all, and she looked me in the eye and said that it was a piece of misogyny, and I didn't deny it. The harridan wife waiting offstage. An old joke.

Yes, I said agreeably, he's pussy-whipped, it's a comic tradition. I'd been working hard and wasn't in the mood for gender equity.

That made her smile, and observe that she had piqued me. I observed that I didn't write the play so it wasn't my misogyny. I tried to read the tag on her plump chest, but couldn't quite. Dick Burkwitz interrupted to hand me a cheque and thank me for the performance, but she didn't go away, just hung about nearby. I put the cheque in my bag and set off for the gym where I would find showers, but she intercepted me. I explained that I had to wash the butter out of my hair, and she laughed companionably, as if we were old friends now, and announced that she would wait for me by the front door, and when I had finished my shower, dressed, there indeed she was sitting on a bench, wearing a coat of fire-engine red to complement the orange hair and purple mouth.

Well, you're not impossible to look at. That's what she said

when I arrived *in propria persona,* and then she asked me where I
wanted to have dinner. I wasn't altogether convinced that any of
this was happening as she accompanied me to my car, instructed
me in the left and right and left again business, and before I knew
it I was in her room in a small private hotel and she was pulling
down my trousers.

Then wrapped in a green silk dressing gown printed with gold
and black dragons, she telephoned out for Chinese, and having
replenished my electrolytes I drove off into the night.

Surely none of this really happened, I thought, as I climbed on
my mattress. I slept like the dead. In the morning I woke recalling
nothing, then suddenly a tumult of memories descended like a
flock of rapacious gulls on a sea of little fishes, stirring the waters
and gobbling furiously. Like the Bacchae falling upon Pentheus,
tearing raw flesh. I rose naked from my mattress and called the
hotel, but she was gone.

The rain pours down, streets awash with running water, the snow
melting away. Tomorrow, my little radio says, it will be cold again.
Winter, spring, winter. I stand in the church and listen to the noise
of rain driven against the windows by an east wind.

The laptop I dropped off for repair the day I performed the
Chekhov has been put in working order, enough money left from
Dick B's cheque to purchase a cheap printer. Next thing I'll be hooking
up to the internet again. We used to share an address, Laura
and I, but now I can have my own – deconsecrations@hotmail.com.
When I phone for technical support and get an Indian-accented
voice, I will ask where my helper lives and if he has seen my lost
wife.

In the evenings I study my old copy of *Our Town*. I find a few
ancient notes in pencil written in the margins, though for the
school production I had a second working copy, pages pasted in a
three-ring notebook with room for lighting cues, blocking, passing
thoughts. A lot of lines to memorize for the Stage Manager, I
notice, and no cues to speak of, no conversations that carry

themselves when Penelope or Jerome or Stanley or Maud says something provoking, and it's pretty clear what you must say in reply. Well, I had the Chekhov to give me practice. Monologues. Funny thing how I end up talking to the audience all the time. Type casting, is it? Fella babbling away and never listening to anyone else.

Hard to catch the tone of the Stage Manager, to know just what tone to catch. Is the play a sentimental idealization of middle-class life? There's the choirmaster who drank and hanged himself, of course. And there's the business about how human beings never realize life when they live it, except maybe the saints and poets. Still there's a kind of generalized quality to the play, a Sunday-school, greeting-card agreement to accept the look of things as the truth of them. Norman Rockwell is the name that gets attached to that set of attitudes. Polish Town – all the foreigners who work in the factories – stands on the other side of the tracks, and only the doctor goes there. The French Canadians live out of sight. The same sort of community when you find it in Sherwood Anderson or Edwin Arlington Robinson shows up with more pain and irony and mess and altogether less niceness. I suppose somehow that Stage Manager, with all his cracker-barrel charm, has to carry the more dire possibilities somewhere behind his words. Every single thing he tells the audience leaves out something else that there's no time to tell them or maybe no way to tell them.

I never said any of these things to Miles Bynner when he was playing the part. He was stiff on stage, and you didn't want to tell him anything that might make him worry and get even more uncomfortable. Tessa, you could tell her anything, so long as you didn't say too much at once, make her try too hard. Just give her time and suggest this and that and she'd make her own way through. Intuitions came from somewhere to guide her. I wonder how all these things I'm thinking about will fit with her conception of the play. Or will she have one? A sharp mind, but not much given to generalizing or theories from what I've seen. She'll know how to guide some local high school girl through Emily's experience, and maybe find ways to give a bit of particularity to the two families who carry the action.

When does the play take place? 1901–1910, sure, but the Stage Manager knows it's a play, and that the doctor died in 1930, so the SM exists in the present, whenever that is – 1938 for the first production or the years of the new millennium for us next summer. How do I dress? I think it has to be 1938. Before the Holocaust and Hiroshima, the civil rights movement and Vietnam and long before the internet and Rwanda and Iraq and all the regular hell of the years since. If the Stage Manager knows those things it's because he has some kind of magic foresight. Wilder says he has a pipe. Well, maybe.

Knows more than he says, that's the key to it, I suspect.

The lawn of Mary Bennett's house is, as every spring, covered with the tiny blue flowers of scilla, the thin stems bent a little with the weight of the bloom, dozens of them, a scattering at random, like fragments of sky, as if some aerial divinity bursting with seed had evacuated his sac in monumental spurts all over this wide space of earth, a promiscuous fertility. My youth, when I splattered semen over Laura's round white breasts, and when we might have conceived a dozen young if we had not been prudent and content with pleasure and gifted with the assistance of modern medicine. She dropped a pill a day and my incessant inseminations came to nothing. The young are born to breed and breed, itching for conjunction at all hours.

That spread of tiny sky-blue flowers makes me think of an Eden, the spare, temporary northern Eden, not the tangled jungle growth where Laura's elephant parts the vines and crushes the orchids beneath his heavy feet.

Once I saw an umbrella stand made from an elephant's foot.

A great thundering on the church doors, Gabriel coming to announce the day of judgement you'd say, and I scurry up to respond, and when I open the door, it is a grey sort of morning, and a young man, his truck at the curb, engine running, holds a

pot of flowers in his hand. He says my name, and I agree that's
who I am, and he offers the flowers. I ask who from, and he advises
me to look for a card, but there is none, and he hasn't the slightest,
but I have to agree that I am Warren Thouless, and he says it's his
bounden duty to hand me this pot of pretty white blooms, forced
paperwhites is what they are. Mistaking the pleasant young man
for an omniscient deity, I ask why someone sent me flowers, and he
says it must be the holiday. What holiday? I say, and it appears
that this is Maundy Thursday and the weekend is Easter. I thought
I was keeping track of things but failed again.

Back indoors I stand about with the pot in my hand, uncertain
where to put it. The little table is taken up with the laptop and
printer and a couple of library books; I am typing out a few
paragraphs as background for my performance in *Our Town*. I
wonder about the top of the trunk, then balance the pot on the
windowsill in front of the frosted glass, and wonder who sent the
pretty things. I doubt that Laura has access to the kind of florist
who ships flowers to other continents. I think of her as if ... well, as
if nothing had changed, the bad message never come through. I go
down the list of possible donors – the dabchick with orange hair
and crimson mouth, Busy Bill, Ms Niles of Toronto, Griff – and
decide on Tubby Bert and his handsome spouse. I could ask, but I
like to remain in doubt.

Bright morning, and I make my way around the lawn of the church
picking up the winter's garbage, pulling leaves away from the
foundation with my gloved fingers. I hesitate to spend money on a
rake. I reach the garden beside the door where I am pulling away
handfuls of leaves and finding the green noses of daffodils seeking
light when I see Barry Engelhart's great-aunt making her slow way
down the hill to her Sunday assignation. I stand and wait for her to
arrive, ready to be friends, hoping not to put my foot in my mouth.
She unsettles me.

'He is risen,' she says when she gets close. How am I to
respond? Congratulations? Glad to hear it?

'Happy Easter,' as I say, as about the best I can manage.

'I just found some daffodils coming up.'

'You got the flowers I sent?'

'It was you. There was no card.'

'And you thought it was some pretty young girl.'

'Pretty young girls don't celebrate Easter. I thought it was Bert Cummings. They're very beautiful.'

'Don't want to come along to church, do you? It's only that United, but it's Easter, after all.'

'I don't think I will. But it's a kind invitation.'

She was walking away.

'Thanks for the flowers,' I shout after her. She doesn't look back.

He is risen, she said. Whatever that meant. I'd been taken to church now and then as a small boy, and I'd heard the story, but it never made a whole lot of sense to me. Nice story in its way, a reassurance that something didn't die, whether or not it was that carpenter's boy who kept getting into trouble, an introspective bachelor with a grand sense of himself, who couldn't stop talking about the kingdom of god, everything he looked at delivering sermons, allegory triumphant.

White flowers catch the light through frosted glass. Whiteness fading into whiteness, flower into frost, pallor into pallor.

Bed. Darkness. Insomnia. Tessa wants to do a Sunday evening reading of *The Duchess of Malfi*. No charge.

First Executioner. As Tessa kneels he winds the rope round her long delicate neck, and with Second Executioner, one on each side, tugs until she is throttled. Why Tessa should wish to play the Duchess of Malfi is a mystery, an astonishment for a dark night like this, silence all around and another silence within, the silence of no-meaning, mind veering hopelessly from memory to fantasy to obsession. The Duchess is a boy actor dressed to kill. Girl playing boy playing girl, Tessa will cut short her hair to do a boyish reading of the part. So she says.

Who do you talk to when you're alone? No one, only keep up the noise: daydream, chimera, nightmare, hallucination. The *D of*

M has what Verdi demanded from his libretti, strong situations. The duke, her twin, whipped by his incestuous desire for her, demands she remain unmarried, and she swears she will, then seduces the first man to cross her path, thrusting the ring on his finger. She breeds apace. Later the ducal twin will come to her – in darkness to avoid catching a glimpse, having sworn never to see her again. He leaves her clutching a dead hand, and then sends a masque of madmen. Strong situations. Then comes First Executioner and wraps her pretty neck in cord. I imagine Laura lying throttled by a couple of professional murderers.

Enough. I climb from the mattress, wrap my naked body in the swallowtail coat for warmth and my feet in shoes to walk about the big empty Sunday-school room, don't bother tying them, wander in the hopeless darkness, windows suddenly illuminated by the headlights of a passing car, a man driving home in the small hours after an assignation with his mistress. It is very quiet. I am alone. I try to count the months since Laura's elephant postcard arrived, but I have lost track of the calendar. When I try to think of her I can only remember the telepathic message invading my brain, the speech of silence. If I go up into the body of the church perhaps I will find a way to pray for her. A silent prayer to the silent. A scrabbling under my feet, Monsieur Rat searching under the boards for food or a nesting place. I speak him good evening and the scrabbling ends. I feel my way along the wall until I come to the stairs, unwilling to turn on the light though I cannot think why. I have stumbled part of the way up the stairs when I realize that I am stepping on a loose shoelace, and I know I am about to fall, and in spite of an exact vision of what is happening to me I can't stop the overbalancing of my body's weight, can only make a helpless noise, and I come down on my hip on the side of the stairs, a noise of pain, the arms I throw out to stop my plunge useless, and my head strikes the floor, all my weight comes down on my back. I am momentarily unconscious, then aware but unable to move and beginning to shiver. I struggle to breathe, and at last draw a few sharp breaths which come with pain. My head is dizzied and I am afraid that if I try to stand I'll faint. I roll on my side, then on my hands and knees, and crawl through the darkness toward the mattress where I can abandon myself to unconsciousness. As I crawl I am seized once more by the wordless voice that comes from far off, and yet while it speaks to me I cannot make out what it wants to say. In the forest schools the newly wise are practising the disciplines of attendant silence. I am pulling the covers over me. The elephant stands guard. I think the telephone is ringing, but I can't rise to get there.

Everything is specific, but nothing is unique. I pass by daffodils and the first tulips, pure colours in the cool spring afternoons, flowers of a cold Eden, at once luminous and bleak. As I walk along the street my injured back is stabbed by invisible knives, and threatens to lock into a spasm of pain, but I hold myself upright and continue to place my feet on the pavement. If I told anyone about my fall they would urge me to drive to the hospital, see doctors. I prefer not. In the drug store on the main street I found a hot water bottle, and before I lie down I fill it from the sink and it offers my back some little comfort. This morning I stood naked in front of the mirror and bent my head around to observe the bruises, and they are large and splendid.

Thundering at the church door again. I suppose the size of them, double wooden panels filling the stone arch, the look of ancient iron hinges, causes people to beat upon them with the enthusiasm of a drunken percussionist. Or perhaps I don't hear until they pound their fists. I struggle upward, my back still painful when I climb stairs, and I open the door, and there in the gentle rain is a handsome man in late middle age, in dirty jeans, thick hair roughly chopped off, with garden shears from the look of it, and at his feet spotted with raindrops, a piece of furniture. At the curb an old half-ton, window open, a German shepherd with its head out watching suspiciously lest I launch an attack on its master. I feel I ought to know the man, but don't.

'Bob Niles,' he says, to help me out, and it comes to me that this is Tessa's father, but his moustache is gone, and it's been

69

years since the night I met him at the school.

I put out my hand, and he shakes it vigorously, which hurts my back, but I try not to flinch.

'Tessa told me I should bring this round when I was down this way,' he says, pointing his thumb toward the piece of furniture, which when I examine it proves to be a small chest of drawers painted black. 'It's been sitting in the barn for a while now.'

I recall a moment in the bar in Toronto when I had tried to amuse the continuity girl by explaining how I lived with my clothes in cardboard boxes. Said it was convenient when it was time to go to the laundromat, just picked up the boxes and put them in the car, folded clothes back into them as they came out of the dryer, and carried them home again. Tessa had obviously listened and decided to do something about me.

'You don't need it?' I said.

'No way on this earth do we have need of it.' North Carolina was still there, quietly, in the background of his words.

'It's good of you to bring it round.'

'She'd be on my case something furious if I didn't.'

'Neither one of us is going to stand in the road of Tessa getting what she wants.'

'You'd be right about that.'

'I don't know why I'm keeping you out there in the rain,' I say. 'Let's bring it in.'

He picks it up, and I hold the door while he lifts it over the sill.

'Where do you want it?'

'Just leave it here for now. I'll take it downstairs later.'

I know that if the two of us carry it down, I'll start yelping when my back hurts, and I figure I'll avoid the embarrassment, yelp in private later on. Bob Niles glances around the bare cold space of the church.

'We were out visiting Jennie's people last year when you were doing your play here. Never saw it.'

'Come this summer.'

'She said you'd be back at it this year.'

From outside we can hear the dog barking.

'I'd better go shut that dog up.'

'Thanks for bringing it round. I didn't bother with furniture much when I sold off the house.'

'I know the feeling. Some days seems it would be easiest to burn the place down and walk away.' I'm startled by his understanding. He nods and is gone, and I look at my new possession, wonder if it's something left over from Tessa's childhood out there in the woods. I also wonder how I'm going to get it downstairs, decide to fetch the heavy maroon curtain I use as a bedspread on cold nights and slide it down on that. Upside down. This takes some time and brings on some yelping, but I get it to the bottom of the stairs and set it by the door of the kitchen. Pile a few books on top, nearby the old trunk, my chair and table, a plug convenient for the laptop.

I sit myself down on the chair for a little rest and contemplation, pick up the first book that comes to hand. *The Cherry Orchard*. I recall the August afternoon when Tessa and Smiler, our little summer adventure concluded, packed the last of their things and set off for Toronto, a hot humid day, and afterward I stood alone in the empty church and felt myself like old Firs at the end of the play, when everyone is gone, Madame Ranevskaya and her brother having said goodbye to the family property where they spent their childhood, left it all behind, the axes chopping down the cherry trees heard from offstage, and then suddenly the sick old man appears. In the excitement of departure nobody has thought of him, and now he lays himself down in the locked building, waiting to be found. Belatedly Tessa decided they should have cast me as Firs, instead of the young man who wore heavy makeup and bound his knees to stiffen them, and even so was unconvincing.

I put my clothes in the shallow drawers and pile the boxes in a corner. Life has gone by, old Firs says to himself, as if I had never lived.

'Griff,' I'm saying, 'It's your fretful father.'

'And how are you?'

'Worried. Have you heard from Laura?'

'No. Haven't you?'

'Not for months.'

'You think there's something wrong.'

'I think she's dead. I think some guru has murdered her for the little spare change in her pockets.'

'You exaggerate. You always exaggerate.'

'Why doesn't she write to you? She's left me behind, well that's OK, maybe she was bored with me after all those years, but you're her son. Her only child. Surely if she was alive she'd send you a note now and then.'

'She thinks I don't understand.'

'She's probably right.'

'Of course she's right. An old woman running off to some ashram in a strange country. It's ridiculous.'

'There's nothing wrong with ridiculous. It would do you good to be ridiculous now and then.'

'We're not talking about me.'

'Maybe you should contact the embassy there. You have friends in the diplomatic corps.'

'One friend, and he's in Norway.'

'You must be able to do something. I'm worried. Aren't you?'

'I wouldn't know where to start.'

'Find her, Griff. Make sure she's OK.'

My agent, it appears, has a DVD of my scene with Tessa from the TV thing, and by means of that she's got me a one-line bit in the American movie that's currently shooting, and I'm on my way to Toronto, unshaven for three days, which is one of the requirements. A long slow morning, makeup people working on my nose and lower lip until I look a good deal worse than usual. Finally get in front of the camera, open a door, face the lens and deliver my one line and slam the door. Never do see the movie star I'm supposed to be addressing, but the director shoots three takes, says OK, and they remove the makeup and I pull my electric razor out of my bag and deal with the whiskers. When I was very small I believed that my father, with his lather and safety razor, was shaving the whispers off his face.

Meet Tessa for a late lunch. She is rehearsing a revival of *The Crackwalker*, plays the dim girl with the baby. As we sit waiting for our food, she tosses on the table a clipping from one of the big papers: Tessa Niles as Artistic Director of the Old Church Theatre Summer Season announces, etc. You're artistic director now are you? I say, and she explains that Smiler has moved west, good parts in Calgary, and after that Vancouver, plans to stay for a while, so she appointed herself, knew I wouldn't mind. Besides, the theatre owes me, she says, after what I went through to get that story, and I tell her to spare me the details, but she doesn't. In the middle of her account of what went on with the journalist in question, I tell her she's treating me like her best girlfriend and get a funny look. She shrugs, quits.

Who is the Stage Manager? she asks suddenly and I look puzzled. Or so I assume. I feel puzzled. She tries again, and I ask if she means that he's the chorus, what the chorus would be in a Greek play. She stares at me for a while and says she was thinking maybe he was god. I am quick to dispute this. All he does is notice things. Well, she says, that's all gods do, notice things.

We eat up, and she departs for rehearsal.

Years ago I was told a silly joke about two elephants playing bookends but I can't quite remember it. I wonder if anyone has published a book of elephant jokes where I could look it up. A friend once came upon two zoo elephants who appeared to be preparing to mate. She waited for an hour for the massive coupling to occur, but though the female was roused and receptive, the bull never quite got to it.

The orchard is blossoming again. This weekend Tessa finishes the run of her play and next week moves down here and starts auditioning kids. She's renting a bedroom from her friend Mara. The Great Dane. One thing she's going to do, I decide, is help me lift up the stove and put in chunks of wood to replace the Book of

73

Common Prayer. Then she can start being artistic director. I've
learned my lines for the first two acts of the Wilder play. Found a
volunteer to run the box office, Annette Zelikovics from the
hairdresser's. Talked her into it while she was cutting my hair. I
called a plumber, who is coming to put in a shower stall
downstairs. Brad Bauer, the local handyman, roughed out the walls
in the space next to the little toilet. A treat for me and for the
actors. Well, one actor at a time, but it's better than nothing. A lot
of complaints from the performers last year about the lack of mod
cons, but now I'm getting it all in order. Downright homey. Brad
knocked together a couple of six-foot-high cubicles for dressing
rooms. I borrowed a hammer from him and nailed up a broomstick
across a corner of my kitchen-bedroom. A place to hang my
swallowtail coat and my winter jacket and a couple of shirts so
maybe the wrinkles will disappear. Or so I hope.

All this to be paid for by my one line in the movie of the week.

'Who was that answered the phone?'

'Tessa.'

'So she is there with you after all.'

'We're rehearsing. I'm performing, and she's directing me.'

'I'll bet she is.'

'What is it you're phoning about, Griff.'

'I called Manfred Gertler.'

'Who's that?'

'My friend at the embassy in Norway. I told him that mother
had disappeared, and asked him if he knew anyone at the embassy
in India.'

'Did he?'

'An old girlfriend of his works there, as a cultural officer.'

'Did he get in touch?'

'By e-mail. And she called him back.'

'So will they go looking for Laura?'

'She said there's no evidence of anything wrong. A woman has
a perfect right to go off and live a new life, even if we don't like it.'

'But she doesn't get in touch.'

74

'No reason she should. That's what she said.'

'Did you tell him that wasn't good enough?'

'If they were going to make any enquiries, I'd have to know exactly where she is.'

'Don't you?'

'I lost the envelope from the letter she sent, and there's no return address on the letter.'

'You should have kept the envelope.'

'It wasn't a mailing address anyway. Just the name of a place. Some long name I don't remember. I thought she'd write again. She didn't give you her address, did she?'

'There's an elephant on her postcard. That's the best I can do.'

'I don't think that's good enough.'

'She might have said the name of a town, when she first told me she was going, but I can't really remember either. I was in a state of shock at the time.'

'I suppose.'

'So they won't look for her.'

'India's huge. A subcontinent. Millions of people there. Thousands of towns and villages. They can't keep track of everybody.'

'I'm not sure she mentioned the place. I just can't remember. I didn't really believe what she was telling me.'

'It's the only way they'll know where to look.'

'I'll search my failing memory.'

'I'll let you get back to your rehearsal.'

'I think it's over. We were nearly finished, and Tessa seems to have wandered off.'

'Let me know if you remember anything.'

'Thanks for trying, Griff.'

The librarian had searched the reference section for the best atlas in the collection, and now he observed with a certain bemusement, Warren Thouless, his old history teacher, examining one of the maps from close up, as if to find some hidden presence in the fine detail of the distant geography. As Warren worked his way over the map, he was once more mumbling to himself. Damn sad, the librarian thought again. He had considered the local gossip about Warren's wife, how a year ago she set off to India seeking spiritual enlightenment. The librarian did not believe this story. Spiritual enlightenment is an empty phrase, so far as he is concerned, at best a kind of auto-intoxication. He believed that Warren's wife had more likely gone off with another man. Or woman. Concealing her actions in the far-fetched story about a distant ashram.

After Warren left the library he was observed at Christy's store picking up some tins of things for his supper. Bun Christy tried to be friendly and made a joke about the pretty young woman who was living with Warren up at the church, another, more recent, item of local gossip. Warren took the joke in good part and explained how in fact she lived elsewhere, etc., etc. Bun Christy looked at the man leaving the store and wondered. The girl was certainly good-looking. Bun wouldn't have kicked her out of his bed if he found her there.

Tessa is doing auditions, planning to cast all the kids and the walk-ons locally. The professionals arrive later on. In the meantime she and I work on the Stage Manager's monologues. In the afternoon she arrives on the bicycle she bought second hand, and wanders about the church listening as I make my way through the lines, now and then pushing me to a different spot on the stage, and she's usually right. She asks me questions that turn the monologue into a temporary dialogue with her, my first audience, and that too is helpful, her listening altering my sense of the words.

Late in the day we are working on the final monologue, and afterward, as the sun begins to strike the westerly windows, we go downstairs for a glass of wine, me sitting on my straight chair, Tessa on top of the trunk with her legs folded in that easy way young women have, bending themselves this way and that, limber as kittens, and after the first glass we have a second glass, and somehow I find that I am mentioning to Tessa that she is sitting on my mother. It's one of those nifty lines you can't resist after two glasses of wine, but now I have to explain about the ashes in the trunk, how after you've waited a month it gets harder to make a decision during the second month, and so on until it's years, and then it's really impossible. The whole thing has become too significant, and so you wait more years. Tessa of course asks the obvious friendly question: where would my mother have liked to be? And I have to say I don't know. I tell her I've been thinking of the river, and she says we could take them out on the lake toward sunset; that would be beautiful, and when I ask how we would get them out on the lake she has an answer. Casey's canoe. Means nothing to me, until Tessa reminds me, and I achieve some dim recall of Casey McIntyre. Never in one of my classes. Track and field. An old chum of Tessa's, it emerges, and he has a little cabin down by the water and has offered her the use of his canoe, which is underneath, chained to the foundation, told her where the key is hidden.

So here I am, better (or worse) by two glasses of wine, and I have to say yes or no to this project. If I say yes, I'll have Tessa's help and encouragement, and if I don't do it now I may die with the ashes hidden away somewhere, and that thought is enough to make up my mind. We arrange to meet down by the wharf, and she goes off on her bicycle, and I open the trunk, move Laura's baby photographs and lift the metal container. It's just ashes, but it is my mother, or what's left of her, and I'm about to dump her in Lake Ontario.

'I have to put them somewhere,' I say out loud, as if in response to my mother's usual stoic silence.

So I drive down to the wharf and park the car, and just along the shore I see Tessa dragging the canoe over the pebbly beach, and with the box of ashes tucked under my arm I go along to meet her there. The bow of the canoe is in the water, and Tessa, who's wearing black jeans and a black shirt, barefoot, jeans turned up, her running shoes lying on the beach nearby, stands waiting, pale, precise features, dark hair, long white toes on the grey stones, like some symbolic figure from an old Bergman movie, a youthful figure in black who is at once Eros and Thanatos, sex and death.

Without words, she indicates that I should get in front with the ashes. There is a paddle leaning against the thwart, and I am reflecting on what a long time it is since I've knelt in a canoe. Tessa will steer, and I discover what I've never till now been aware of, that there is a small lake adjacent to the little hippie farm, and from childhood Tessa learned to be right smart in a canoe. So much we never know.

She pushes off and we begin to paddle out into the lake. Far off I can see the low black shape of a freighter, and the sun is dropping toward the horizon. Close to shore, the curving shape of a sail, catching the tiny bit of breeze that ripples the path in front of us. I paddle automatically, and the boat rides off into a summer evening years ago when I paddled over the still water of a lake among pines. The canoe is steered by the stern paddle, and my only job is to make way through the gradually deepening water. I have read in the newspapers that with the pollution reduced the lake trout are beginning to spawn again. Young fish have been seen. Deep down the lake sturgeon live their dark ancient lives, and my mother's ashes will fall into that blank eternity of slow geological time.

We are moving away from shore, and I wonder how much further to go. Perhaps this is far enough. I take my paddle from the water and set it down beside me, take up the metal box and open it. Wordless in the face of this final action. My mother is long gone. Laura is gone. I take a handful of the ashes, shocked at the cold rubbly touch and I toss them toward the setting sun. They catch the angled light and then strike the water, a scintillation of brilliance as they come down like a rain of fire, sizzling and vanishing. For a moment I believe that this is Laura's body I am committing to the deep, and at the same time I believe that Laura is the invisible presence behind me, propelling the boat outward, away from land, and yet I know both these things are untrue. Yet she is here, somehow, even if she is far off, even if she is dead. Another handful of ashes, and another, and finally I tilt the container and the last fall into the lake, and I dip the box and rinse it with water until the very last bits of her are gone. I am humming a tune to myself as I do it, but I can't remember why I know the notes or if they once had words. I set the box in the front of the canoe and take hold of the paddle. I push it through the water, and the boat begins a long slow turn across the light wind, and Tessa directs our course back to land where we will draw the canoe ashore, lock it to the foundation of the cabin and walk up to the pizzeria for dinner.

The Lion complained to Jupiter that though he was fierce and strong, with teeth and claws, he was frightened by the crowing of a cock. Jupiter explained to him that every creature fears something. One day the Lion met an elephant and observed how his ears were always in motion, flapping and trembling. The elephant, he learned, was afraid of the gnats that flew about his head. If one was to enter his ear, he believed, it would be the death of him. This, according to Aesop, made the lion feel much better.

When Griff was little someone gave him a kit out of which he made a cardboard elephant, by cutting and folding the pattern. Then one summer a boy who was visiting a grandmother just down the street stole it. Or so we believed. At any rate it was gone, and Griff was heartbroken.

The elephant postcard rests inside one of the copies of the Book of Common Prayer that Tessa helped me rescue, at the page where there is to be found the order for the burial of the dead. *Man that is born of woman*, etc.

Who first said that the elephant is wise? That he never forgets?

Tessa has created a poster on Mara's up-to-date computer. I get it photocopied, and between rehearsals I make a poster run through the countryside, following the same route as last year, stopping everywhere to chat about the play and mentioning to all I meet the local kids who'll be appearing. One of same gets recruited to poster the main street.

We've arranged to meet for coffee and a gab at Tim's after Bert has finished work, and I arrive just as the rain is setting in for a serious attack, and two minutes later Bert ambles across the parking lot,

79

comes through the door, folds his umbrella, and as he approaches the table holds out to me a good-quality yellow slicker. Doesn't suppose that I have one, not having most of what I need. I hope he isn't including brains in that. It appears that this excellent garment has been lying around in the lost and found at the Township Hall for months, and today, noticing the rain outside his window, Bert has decided to award it to me for cultural services to the township. In return I invite him to attend, free of charge, the dress rehearsal of *R Town*, and he says he'll give it some thought. So we chatter, and the rain sets in for a serious downpour, big drops beating the earth, forming puddles and then hurling themselves against the surface to create little waterspouts. Waves pouring down the glass windows. Men and women arrive in the coffee shop shaking like dogs to dry themselves.

The rain is still teeming when Bert decides it is time to go home and let June feed him up, and thinking about his kindness I scuttle to the car, grateful in the shelter of my new garment. I drive more or less blind up to the church, windshield wipers sweeping back and forth in the sheets of water, each sweep providing an only momentary view of the street. I park out back, and pull up my hood to make a break for the side door. As I run I notice Tessa's bike lying on the lawn, abandoned. Assume she has ridden through this deluge on her way here, and when I open the door, everything is quiet, no lights turned on, and in the dim rainlight I see her sitting on one of the straight chairs on the stage, her sodden T-shirt on the floor beside her, pale skin as Mara stands behind the chair and dries her hair with my striped bath towel. Mara is a strapper, tall and big-boned, hawk-nosed, and Tessa in her care looks small and young. As the door closes I am – Tessa's idea of god – noticing things, the tableau of two figures, shapes of pewter and ivory and ebony in the gloom. Their heads turn toward me. This is one wet girl, Mara announces, and wraps the towel around the wet girl's straight, slender shoulders, and the wet girl asks if she might borrow some clothes, and I tell her to help herself, and off she goes downstairs, and Mara observes that she was half drowned cycling through the storm. Tessa returns in one of the shirts I had hung in the corner of the room and a pair of baggy pants that evoke phony cigars and pratfalls, her dark hair sticking out in all directions. *Quel outfit*, Mara says, and I agree, and Tessa does a little comic dance and bows, a comedian from silent film making you laugh and breaking your heart.

The two young ladies are going out for dinner, and they invite me to come along, but I say I am counting on a feed of salami fried in onions and rice boiled up with tinned tomatoes and cayenne, and nothing else will satisfy me, so I lend Tessa my new slicker, and off they go in Mara's car, a stop for real clothes and then a night on the town. The church is silent after they leave.

When Tessa returns my clothes, they are not only washed, but ironed. That girl was brought up right, I guess. After school I have my first rehearsal with Krista Crawford, the schoolgirl who's to be our Emily. Tessa, for reasons still obscure to me, wants her to start with the dead scene, Tessa reading Mrs Gibbs since Jayn Mumford isn't here yet.

A call from Bert. I have mentioned to him that Barry Engelhart's great-aunt comes past now and then, and he is calling to tell me that she is in hospital, incapacitated by a stroke. Ninety years old apparently. The wheel goes round. I plan to visit once the play is open. She can't speak, but one supposes she can hear and comprehend. Two months ago she sent me flowers. I get on the blower and arrange for some to be sent to her, and while I'm at it I send some to Tessa at Great Daneville. Why not?

An unsigned postcard from somewhere in the USA. On the front a photograph of baboons with their haughty blue faces and hot red backsides. The message is in some script I don't comprehend, possibly Russian, and I assume it is from the bright creature who boarded and pillaged me after my Chekhov impersonation. No doubt a quotation from Anton P. But how did she get my address? Or maybe without knowing it I have become part of a Russian spy ring. If they still have Russian spy rings.

Who do you talk to when you're alone? I'm never alone. We're in rehearsal now, all the actors on site, and the church is never empty. When it isn't the cast it's Bernie Boccaloni setting up towers of scaffolding and hanging lights. The designer has sent a list of what instruments he wants and Bernie comes in after work to do the job, hanging lights and taping cables. What with the local casting, and the fact that we've come back for a second year, we have a lot more involvement by the neighbours. Annette Zelikovics has worked out a seating system involving colour coding, so while the seats are unnumbered, they are sold at two different prices. Mara gathers the cast for music rehearsals the last half hour of the day, teaching them the hymns and the actor playing Simon Stimson how to beat time, and then some of them hang around drinking beer or pop and kibitzing, two of them going off into a corner to run a scene. Brett Zemans, who's playing Dr Gibbs, arrives before anyone else in the morning, sometimes before I'm up, with a container of some hideous vegetarian breakfast drink, veggies and seeds and yoghurt and seaweed put through the blender and imbibed from a large plastic container with a snap-on lid, and after he chokes that down, he spreads his little rubber mat in a corner to do yoga. I've told him that yoga is forbidden here, but it does no good. He just smiles and goes on with his stretching and bending and slow breathing. I've dealt with all this crowding by going to Wimpy's Used Clothing and picking up a dressing gown, so I no longer stagger naked to the little bathroom and the new shower stall, and I've rearranged my little room to accommodate, not without difficulty, the dresser and my little table and chair, everything contained behind one door, and I can close the door and mumble and fart without interruption. To make space I had to move out the plastic garbage container and the broom, which now stand by the bottom of the stairs, and the garbage bin soon gets full of everybody's leftover lunch, and I have made announcements about this, to little purpose. By the far wall of the Sunday school room there is a table with a cheap mirror above it, and two chairs in front – makeup, for the putting on of. The phone is a problem. It rings at unsuitable times, interrupting rehearsals, so we are

having a second jack installed, downstairs, in the corner that
Annette is turning into a business office – another table and chair,
and we have hired an answering service, more expense. Apparently
we are getting enquiries about tickets, as if people might actually
wish to attend the play. Tessa has had to turn down a part in a
movie and says she'll need a raise. Since she is paying her own
salary until ticket sales take off, I say she can double it. A small
bank loan is paying the salaries of the other actors. I try not to
think about money. How many theatres can operate without
paying rent? We're ahead that way. Besides, I'm an artist, I tell
myself, as I rehearse each afternoon. Let someone else be producer
and finance officer and general manager and dogsbody. Who?
After rehearsals I go for a walk in the orchard up and down
between the rows of overgrown, unpruned trees, to clear my head,
and sometimes Tessa comes with me, and one day I tell her I have
a serious question, and I ask her if her dog still eats nuts, and she
reassures me that it does. The next day she wears the shirt and has
to explain it to everyone.

Bernie Boccaloni has finished hanging the lights and has begun
putting up the curtains that we pull across the church windows,
since the summer evenings are long and luminous. Bernie is at his
best high in the air.

Tessa is being interviewed by a local newspaper. Krista Crawford
who wants to learn about theatre is walking the stage for the
lighting designer. The elephant has followed the monkey into the
treetops but is having trouble hanging on. God's in his heaven
noticing things. I am noticing Bernie Boccaloni noticing Tessa.

Seven in the morning. A pounding on the door of my room.

'Warren, what are you doing in there?'

'Making noises.'

'You sound like you're having the world's longest loudest
orgasm.'

No. I have been using a selection of Laura's noises as a wakeup
exercise and a warmup for my voice. Maybe I think it will create

some link between us and save her life. I rise from the mattress, draw my dressing gown around me, open the door, ask Tessa – who's wearing the My Dog Eats Nuts shirt, crank-turning white shorts, sandals – what she's doing here at this hour, apart from insulting people. She is in a rage with Tom Dembrovich, the lighting designer. He spent so much time on the light cues that they didn't finish the tech they started yesterday evening, though they worked to exhaustion late into the night while I was dead to the world on my mattress – she checked to see – and now Tom's gone off to Toronto for a production meeting for another show, won't be back until tomorrow, the day of the final dress with a small invited audience, and in the middle of all this she comes to me for support and finds me growling and chuntering behind a closed door. I start to explain about Laura's noises and am told to belt up, put on my clothes and take her out for breakfast. On the way out we meet Brett Zemans arriving with his plastic jug of yuck. At Tim's, where men stare at her, she sits in silence, drinks a giant coffee and eats chocolate eclairs. We hold hands for twenty-two seconds and set off back to the church where Tessa borrows a towel, planning to have a scalding hot shower to set her going for the day. The phone is ringing.

Dryness, I remind myself, is what Wilder, in his notes to directors, says is required in the tone of the play. Bone-dry Warren. Feel, in fact, distinctly damp.

Before the dress rehearsal Tessa and Tom D. run the final lighting cues, the ones left over from the unfinished tech. Then a few people arrive to sit in the seats, and we put on our funny clothes and perform for them. I forget my lines once, but otherwise I work it through with a certain conviction. Afterward Tessa gives us a few brief notes and a pep talk. Everyone leaves the theatre, and I go out into the night and look at the orchard in the moonlight. The moon is almost full. Mosquitoes chase me back indoors where I lie naked on my mattress under a single sheet.

* * *

84

Opening night, and we've made it to Act 3. There are people in all the seats. Before each act I check out a page or so from the three-ring binder in which I've recorded little narratives of events during the 1930s, Edmund Wilson on coal strikes in the US, an account of the Regina riot, the Bennett-buggies, Kristallnacht in Germany, and I assume that my lines are somehow informed by everything I know but don't say. I'm got up in white shirt and old-fashioned wool trousers held up by suspenders, and on the surface I am that America stereotype the Cracker-Barrel Philosopher. Whether I'm getting across any more than that, well, who knows? I'm coming to the end of my long spiel at the beginning of the act about the graveyard and those in it, *waiting for the eternal part to come out clear*, I say and a couple of the still-living characters come onstage and I introduce them, pick up a chair and turn it around and straddle it while the scene goes on.

Somewhere at the back of the old church, probably beside the table where the lighting man works the board, Tessa is observing all this, in her dressed-up-director clothes, faded but freshly washed and ironed tight jeans, a shirt of white linen, all but transparent as it hangs over her young breasts, and with it she wears a man's sport coat in a very fine tweed. Looks stylish enough.

There's a full moon tonight. When the wide doors of the church open for the funeral procession, the actors are revealed in silhouette against the blue light of the moon on the sloping lawn. A little sense of crowding, for some reason, as they form up in the darkness and proceed up the centre aisle, carrying the imaginary coffin, not quite the staging in the text, but it works well here where we have no backstage. Tessa has arranged to borrow some canvas flats for the next production, a comedy which demands wings and a crossover. The mourners carry the coffin up to the stage, set it down, and they begin quietly to sing, 'Blessed be the tie that binds,' what they sang at the choir practice two acts earlier.

It's a while before I have any lines. Right now I just watch the action, maybe direct the audience's attention by directing mine, but as I sit here I recall that little bustle of actors arriving at the door, never quite like that before, and I get the idea that there was an extra body in the little crowd. That against the pale moonlight of the outdoors I might have seen a familiar face.

This is the night when, for better or worse, I plan to invite Tessa to join me on the mattress. Our show successfully opened, a warm summer night of the full moon. I cleaned the place up, bought some cut flowers for the little table, orange juice for breakfast. The window open for fresh air, a screen to keep out the mosquitoes.

So who was that by the church door? Some late arrival slipping in to catch the last few minutes of the play? The more I think of it the more I believe – crazy, I know it – that I saw Laura's face back there, for only an instant. Laura has sent her ghost to keep me in order. Don't be a fool, she'll say. You're sixty and that girl is young and beautiful. Comfort, though, we have a right to a little comfort, and the kindly touch of warm skin. You took off on me, Laura, looking for god or whatever. You got yourself murdered in some exotic corner of the big world..

I try to concentrate on the action. Not long until Emily, the dead Emily, will speak to me, and I will tell her about life and death. As if I knew.

I picture the two of them standing at the back of the church, in the darkness, Tessa and Laura's ghost, and they listen to me as I negotiate with Emily her return to earth for just one day, her twelfth birthday. Maybe Laura has negotiated to come back for one night. I retire to my corner of the stage, and the past is played out, Emily living out the moments when she's both dead and alive. I glance out at the audience, looking for that familiar face, but blinded by the stage lighting I can see nothing except a few people who are sitting close up, and I see that in the front row a woman has tears running down her face. The play is not supposed to be sad in that way, but who's to know just what the effect of any performance will be? The woman identifies with something in the action, and it's stirring her up, and as I glance back at the characters on stage it comes to me for the first time that maybe Laura is really here at the back of the theatre. It's not a ghost come

86

to protect me. Laura is alive, has escaped First Executioner and Second Executioner, and she has slipped in out of the moonlight, and she's standing at the back of the church beside Tessa, and afterward she will find me. A visit of two days and she'll be gone again, is that it?

The dead are speaking now, and Emily has come back among them, and as they conclude, instead of drawing a curtain in front of them, as the text indicates, I look toward the lighting board and draw down my hand to cue the slow blackout of the stage except the spot where I'm standing, as I talk about the stars and how late it is, and I wish the audience goodnight. The lighting man pulls the last cue and leaves us in darkness. The audience begins to applaud. In a second the lights will come up again and we will take our bows.

David Helwig was born in Toronto but suffered his teen-age years in Niagara-on-the-Lake. After studying at the University of Toronto and the University of Liverpool he taught at Queen's University. He was involved, along with other young poets including Michael Ondaatje and Tom Marshall, in the publication of *Quarry* magazine, and he created three series of Quarry posters. While in England in 1969–70 he founded the annual Oberon story anthology, which continues to thrive. During the late sixties he taught in Collins Bay Penitentiary and put together a book with one of the inmates there (*A Book About Billie*, 1972). In 1974 John Hirsch hired him to be literary manager of CBC TV Drama, and he worked at the CBC until 1976. In 1980 he left his teaching position at Queen's and from then on earned his living as a freelance writer, writing for television, radio, magazines and newspapers, as well as doing a good deal of editing. He is the author of more than thirty books, mostly fiction and poetry. *Catchpenny Poems* won the CBC poetry award in 1983, and in 2004, his long poem, *The Year One*, won the Atlantic Poetry Award.

Other Books by David Helwig

A prolific author, David Helwig's many publications include:

Atlantic Crossing (1974)
A Book of the Hours (1979)
Catchpenny Poems (1984)
The Bishop (1986)
The Hundred Old Names (1986)
A Postcard from Rome (1988)
Old Wars (1989)
Just Say the Words (1994)
The Child of Someone (1997)
Close to the Fire (1999)
Telling Stories (2000)
The Time of Her Life (2000)
Living Here (2001)
This Human Day (2001)
The Stand-In (2002)
Duet (2004)
The Year One (2004)
The Names of Things (2006)

The cover art is a watercolour on paper, *After Bannerman*, by Sarindar Dhaliwal. It is an element of the installation 'Teepees & Tigers: From One Indian to Another', 1996. Collection the artist.